Codename: Parsifal

A WWII Thriller

Martin Roy Hill

32-32 North

Codename: Parsifal

Copyright © 2023 by Martin Roy Hill

All rights reserved. No part of this book may be used or reproduced in any manner whatsoever without written permission of the author, except in the case of brief quotations used in critical articles or reviews.

Published by

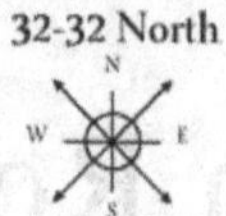

An imprint of

M. R. Hill Publishing

San Diego, California

This book is a work of fiction. Names, characters, businesses, organizations, places, events, and incidents either are the product of the author's imagination or are used fictitiously. Any resemblance to actual persons, living or dead, events, or locales is entirely coincidental.

For information contact:

www.martinroyhill.com

ISBN 979-8-218-182496

Cover Design: RebecaCovers

Books by Martin Roy Hill

Fiction

The Linus Schag, NCIS, Thrillers
The Killing Depths (2012)
The Butcher's Bill (2017)
Upriver (2022)

The Peter Brandt Mysteries
Empty Places (2013)
The Last Refuge (2016)
The Fourth Rising (2020)

The USCG DSF-Papa Thrillers
Polar Melt: A Novel (2019).
Chimera Island (2021)

Standalones
Duty: Stories of Mystery and Suspense from the Cold War and Beyond (2012)
Eden: A Sci-Fi Novella (2014)

Nonfiction
War Stories: Tales of Leadership, Courage, Blunders, and SNAFUs (2018)

PART ONE

The Spear

Chapter 1

Vienna, Austria
March 1938
The Anschluss

STRICTLY SPEAKING, HE WAS an unimpressive-looking man. Of average height and build, with a pale, pinched face adorned with a small triangular mustache above thin, colorless lips, he would not stand out in a crowd, nor was he likely to attract a feminine eye. His thinning hair was cropped tight around the sides and back, in the style of the day, and his rat-like blue-gray eyes maintained their focus with the help of old-fashioned pince-nez lenses.

What made this man stand out was the way he dressed—a pure black uniform jacket accentuated with silver piping, black riding breeches, and gleaming black jackboots. His peaked cap bore the silver death-head skull of the Schutzstaffel or SS, the security apparatus of the German Nazi Party. The pièce de résistance was the embroidered rank bullion on the collar of his jacket that identified him as the leader of the SS, Reichsführer-SS Heinrich Himmler.

Two guards standing at the entrance to the Hofburg Palace in Vienna were also dressed in black, with twin lightning bolt runes on their collars showing they were members of Himmler's SS. They both snapped to attention as soon as they saw Himmler step from his staff car. As he approached the door to the museum, they swung the doors open as one, then stood back with stiff right arms held in salute. "Heil Hitler!" they said in unison.

Himmler ignored them. Carrying a large, black leather briefcase, he entered the museum and, without asking directions, marched straight to the Imperial Treasury room. There was only one guard there, also SS, and he greeted the reichsführer in the same manner as the first two. His attention focused on the only display in the room, Himmler returned the salute with a distracted wave of his right hand and a muttered, "Heil Hitler."

Inside the massive glass case stood a bejeweled cross, glistening with every known gem. Beside it sat a bejeweled crown and a golden orb topped with a cross, also encrusted with gems. A sword in a golden sheath lay in front of these, as if guarding the others. These were the Holy Roman Relics, the royal artifacts that for centuries represented the Holy Roman Empire's Christian sovereignty over much of Europe, from its beginning under Charlemagne until its collapse as the Hapsburg dynasty in the 1800s at the hands of Napoleon Bonaparte of France.

As magnificent as these items were, they held little interest for Himmler. The sight of another relic in the case arrested his attention—the head of a spear about a foot and a half long, and four inches at its widest. Embedded in its dark gray blade was an ancient nail, held in place with wire and a sheath of gold. Stamped into the golden jacket were the Latin words *Lancea et clavus Domini*, or Lance and Nail of Our Lord. This, according to the museum's curators, was the Holy Lance, the spear of a Roman centurion named Longinus, who used it to stab Jesus Christ as he hung lifeless from the cross to determine if he were truly dead. Since the days of Constantine, every Holy Roman emperor carried the spear into battle, earning it the more popular name, the Spear of Destiny.

"You are the only guard on duty here," Himmler said, a statement, not a question.

"Yes, Herr Reichsführer," the guard replied.

"Good. Now leave me."

The guard broke his stiff-back stance to look at Himmler. "Herr Reichsführer?"

"You heard me," Himmler said. He sniffed and added, "I can smell tobacco on your uniform. Go indulge in your filthy habit. I need a few minutes to myself to … contemplate these treasures."

"But Herr Reichsführer," the guard protested. "My hauptmann ordered me to not allow anyone in the treasure room unescorted."

"And who does your hauptmann take his orders from?"

"You, mein Herr," the guard said.

"Exactly," Himmler said. He made a dismissive gesture with his hand. "Now go."

The guard turned to leave, but Himmler barked, "Stop!"

The guard turned and again snapped to attention.

"You have the key to the display case?"

"Yes, Herr Reichsführer," the guard said.

Himmler held out his hand. When the guard didn't respond, he snapped his fingers. "The key." The guard dug the key from his pocket and placed it in Himmler's palm. "Now go."

The guard executed an about face and quick-marched out of the room.

Himmler strode up and down in front of the glass case, waiting until he was certain no one else would disturb him. He used the key to unlock the case and withdrew the spear head. Holding it up to the light, he examined its details, ran his finger over the golden Latin words, pressed his finger against the nail embedded in its blade, and gently touched the tip. After all the centuries, it was still sharp. He had hoped it would be.

The reichsführer had made a study of the Holy Lance. He was convinced the story of its power to lead men to fulfill their destinies was true. So convinced he was of its authenticity, he had a replica made of the spear to display in his office at Wewelsburg Castle, the sacred citadel of the SS. Another he had made to present to Hitler. He had told the Führer that when the time came, he would present the True Spear to Hitler.

Himmler also believed the spear still held the blood of Christ on its tip, however little there may still be left of it. And that was the reason he came to Hofburg Palace as soon as the Anschluss, the German invasion and takeover of Austria, was accomplished. He saw no reason to waste the spear and its powers on Hitler. The Führer held no beliefs in the church and its legends, or in the mysticism Himmler embraced. He, the reichsführer, was far better prepared to employ its powers.

Himmler pressed his left thumb against the spear's point until it pierced the skin. His hand recoiled from the prick. He set the spear down, removed the pince-nez glasses he wore for his near-sightedness, and studied his thumb as a small bubble of blood formed. Carefully placing the spectacles into a pocket, he picked up the Holy Lance again and examined its tip. A small amount of blood smeared the tip, his blood mingling with the blood of Jesus Christ. He looked at his thumb again. Christ's blood mixing with his *inside his veins*.

A curious sensation came over him, a lightheadedness, almost giddiness. He sensed an energy, a power surge inside him. He hadn't expected this. All his life, Himmler felt inadequate. His size, his looks, his poor eyesight, his lack of experience with women. And despite having enlisted in the German Army during the last war, he remained in a reserve unit that never saw action, unlike the Führer, or Göring, or even that scar-faced sybarite Ernst Röhm, head of the Brown Shirts.

But now he sensed a confidence. *He* was the new man of destiny—he felt that now in his heart, felt it in his veins where the blood of Christ flowed with his own. His destiny was now foretold, and he knew he would stand among the other greats who held the spear—Constantine, Charlemagne, and others.

Himmler broke from his reverie and glanced at his pocket watch. It was time to go. He opened his briefcase and removed the twin of the Holy Lance, one of the replicas he had ordered manufactured. He placed it in the case where the True Spear had lain and picked up the real spear. With all the reverence it deserved, Himmler placed the Spear of Destiny into his briefcase and closed it. Then he locked the display case.

With the briefcase gripped tightly, he strode through the museum to the entrance and opened the door. The two outside guards and the guard from inside the Treasury Room snapped to attention. Himmler glanced at his watch again, then addressed the guards.

"The Führer will be here within the hour to examine the Holy Roman Relics," he said. "When he is finished, the relics will be packed—carefully packed, mind you—and transported to Germany. Do you understand?"

"Jawohl, Herr Reichsführer," the three men answered.

"Good," Himmler said. He handed the display case key back to the inside guard and, sniffing the air, added, "I recommend you men refrain from your use of tobacco. The Führer hates that habit more than I do."

After the reichsführer left, the third guard returned to his post in the Treasury Room. He paced the room for several minutes, occasionally opening his tunic and flapping its lapels, hoping to reduce the smell of cigarette smoke. Outside, he heard the arrival of several vehicles and realized the Führer's caravan had arrived.

Quickly buttoning and adjusting his tunic, he took his post next to the display when he noticed a small blotch of red inside the case frame that he was sure wasn't there before. He unlocked the case and studied the blotch. Blood? He turned at a commotion outside the palace door. *The*

Fuhrer! Yanking a handkerchief from his pocket, he wiped the blood and locked the case, stuffed the handkerchief back into his pocket, and snapped to attention.

He waited, but no one entered the room. Curiosity plagued his mind, and he turned to examine the relics. *Did the reichsführer hurt himself on one of the relics?* He looked at the sword, but he was certain it hadn't been moved. His eyes went to the spear head and focused on its tip. *Was that a minute drop of blood on its tip?*

Footsteps echoed outside the room. The guard resumed his rigid posture. Doors burst open and Adolf Hitler entered the room.

Chapter 2

April 1945

On the Outskirts of Frankfurt, Germany

CAPTAIN RAYMOND "MAC" MACAULEY pulled up the collar of his combat jacket as the youth driving the Willys jeep made another suicidal turn around a corner and gunned the engine. The jacket, like the rest of his battle dress, was new, clean, and well-pressed. He wore paratroop wings over his left pocket, and the patch on his shoulder also showed wings, one on each side of a circle in which the letters "SF" were embroidered. The SF stood for Special Forces and the patch represented his membership in that part of the Office of Strategic Services that fought their war behind enemy lines. Around his neck he wore a silk scarf, a symbol many of the members of his elite unit wore when they weren't dodging Germans behind the lines.

Mac wasn't a big man, no more than five-ten, with a slender but sinewy build. He was in his late twenties. His face was sun creased but his tan had faded, the result of spending the last several months in a hospital bed instead of the field. His hair was short and dark, his eyes black hollow caves. Those eyes now took in the town he and the driver were passing through.

There was little left of the town on the outskirts of Frankfurt, Germany. Allied bombers and artillery had reduced most of the buildings to rubble. The driver, a ridiculously youthful blond GI named Smitty or Smithy, dodged around the ruins like a skier on a slalom course.

"Soldier," Mac yelled over the whine of the jeep's engine, "the war's almost over. It'd be a shame if we weren't around to enjoy it."

"Snipers, sir," the soldier replied. "Still snipers around. Slowing down makes us better targets."

Mac glanced at the ruined buildings again as they swept past and realized the kid was right. He tightened his grip on his seat and sighed, "Understood."

"Almost there, sir," the driver said.

A minute later, the vehicle slowed to a stop in front of what had once been a church before bombs and artillery robbed it of its steeple and chased its parishioners away. The church and its surrounding gardens had once been a local attraction, luring Germans from around the country there to worship their Creator and contemplate their sins. Now, the shell-pocked gardens were little more than a parking lot for American jeeps, trucks, staff cars, and half-tracks bristling with antennae and machine guns. An American flag hung above its arched entry. Alongside it waved another flag, smaller and adorned with four gold stars.

MacAuley eyed the smaller flag. "*This* is OSS headquarters?"

"No, sir," said the driver. "This is General Patton's headquarters. This is where I was told to deliver you."

"But my orders are to report to Colonel Fender, regional commander for OSS."

"Colonel Fender has offices here, too," the driver said. "The general likes to keep his friends close, and his enemies closer."

Mac eyed the young man. "Is that supposed to be a joke, soldier?"

"No, sir, simply a statement of fact," the driver said. "And you might want to lower your collar and put on a tie instead of that scarf. The general is a stickler for proper appearance. That, too, is a statement of fact, sir."

MacAuley climbed from the jeep and reached into his B-4 bag and did what the kid suggested. After adjusting the tie, he grabbed the suitcase and started to lift it from the rear of the jeep.

"Never mind that, captain," the driver said. "I'll take that to your quarters. I'll be back here when you're finished with your meeting."

The jeep leapt forward, careened around a corner, and was out of sight. Mac adjusted his necktie again. It felt like a noose around his neck, but he knew—as the kid said—that Patton insisted his soldiers wear neckties whenever not in active combat. He tugged at the bottom of his jacket to straighten it and made sure his pistol belt was properly aligned. Then he removed his overseas cap and ran his fingers through his black, slicked-back hair. The whole process made him feel foolish, like a young boy prepping for his first date. He replaced his cap and trotted up the stairs and went into the church.

The inside of the church hardly looked like a place of worship. MPs—military police—with gleaming white helmets and Thompson submachine guns stood guard in the narthex. Where there had been benches for parishioners, the nave was now crowded with row after row of desks, some standard army field desks, some improvised with wooden crates and planks, some confiscated from nearby bombed-out buildings. The alcoves of the transept were walled off to form small, private offices. The altar was stripped of its religious icons and in their place hung a large wall map.

Mac presented his ID to a guard, who waved him in. He stopped at the first desk in the nave where a young sergeant with a typewriter greeted him with a crisp, "Yes, sir?"

"I'm here to see Colonel Fender," MacAuley said.

"Captain MacAuley?"

"Yes."

"Of course, Colonel Fender and the general are waiting for you, sir," the noncom said. "This way, sir."

"The general?"

"Yes, sir," the young man said. "General Patton."

MacAuley's cheeks puffed out, and he blew air in a silent whistle as he wondered, *What am I in for now?*

MacAuley had never met Patton, but he knew of him. The OSS officer had served in North Africa earlier in the war when Patton commanded the U.S. II Corps. He had also read a profile on Patton the OSS produced in the aftermath of the general's peculiar behavior during the Sicily campaign. There were two separate incidents in which the general slapped GIs being treated for combat fatigue in field hospitals, calling them "cowards." The American press had a field day with that when the story broke. Lesser known was a series of atrocities committed by soldiers under his command.

Prior to the invasion of Sicily, Patton had given a series of hell-fire speeches to his troops imploring them to kill the enemy wherever, whenever, and however. Though warned his fiery rhetoric could be misinterpreted by the soldiers, Patton refused to mitigate his bombast. Unfortunately, the warnings came true. Soldiers of the 45th Infantry gunned down more than a hundred German and Italian POWs as well as Italian citizens before Patton relented and issued orders to stop the slaughter.

Patton also spent more time fighting British Field Marshal Bernard Montgomery than the Germans. The two had been adversaries since the Tunisian campaign. Both men had massive egos and were wartime prima donnas. Patton was also an Anglophobe and disliked the English more than he did the Germans. He and Monty battled each other for ammo, fuel, supplies, and publicity as their troops slugged it out with the enemy on opposite sides of the island. Each general was determined to beat the other to the port city of Messina at the northern tip of the island. Patton won the race. But as the two Allied generals plotted against each other, the Germans pulled off their own version of the Dunkirk Miracle. Over five nights, they secretly evacuated more than one hundred thousand German and Italian troops off the island to mainland Italy, where they would eventually face down the Allied armies again in the bloody slugfest called the Italian Campaign.

Patton's OSS profile included more strange information on the general. Born into a modest, middle-class family, Patton married into wealth. After doing so, he took on many of the attitudes of the upper class—a hatred of communism, socialism, labor movements, and a fondness for the rise of fascism in Europe. Unlike many others in the upper echelons of society, Patton was no Nazi lover; he had killed enough Germans to prove that. But he was openly antisemitic. During one of the slapping incidents in Sicily, several war correspondents heard him yell, "There is no such thing as shell shock. It's an invention of the Jews."

What MacAuley found most bizarre about Patton was his belief in reincarnation. The general openly spoke about being the reincarnation of a Roman soldier. On more than one occasion, he had his driver take him to the location of some ancient battle. Patton would prattle on about the conflict, then conclude that he himself had taken part in the fight. The general had even written a poem about his multiple lives. One stanza still echoed in MacAuley's memory.

So as through a glass, and darkly
The age long strife I see
Where I fought in many guises,
Many names, but always me.

He rallied himself from his thoughts and turned to the sergeant. "This is kind of small for General Patton's headquarters, isn't it?" What he really meant was the church was less opulent than the buildings Patton usually used as his HQ.

"Oh, this is only temporary," the sergeant said. "Third Army is pushing forward so fast, it's hard for us to keep up. But there is an estate a few miles outside this town where we'll set up a permanent HQ. We're just waiting for the current occupants to vacate."

"The current occupants would be …?"

"The German headquarters staff."

The noncom approached a door at the back of the altar and rapped on it twice.

A strangely high pitched, nasally voice on the other side barked, "Enter!"

Opening the door, the sergeant announced, "General, Captain MacAuley is here."

Through the door, MacAuley caught his first glimpse of the man soldiers called "Old Blood and Guts"—General George S. Patton, Jr.

Chapter 3

AT FIFTY-NINE, PATTON WAS edging on the far side of middle-age, with close-cropped white hair that had retreated more than halfway to the back of his scalp. His pale face had a jowly canine quality and wore a permanent scowl. Despite his age, he stood over six feet and ramrod straight. He wore an Ike jacket with several rows of ribbons and four stars on each epaulet, a khaki shirt and tie with matching cavalry riding pants that ballooned at the thighs, and high-laced riding boots. His trademark ivory-handled revolvers hung from his hips. To Mac, Patton looked like someone from a long bygone era.

Nevertheless, he marched into the room, snapped to attention, and saluted. "Captain Raymond MacAuley reporting as ordered, sir."

Patton waved a swagger stick in something of a return salute. "Goddam about time. What took you so damn long?" he demanded. His voice was nasally and high pitched. "You get here by mule train?"

"By Lysander, sir," Mac replied. "England was fogged in."

Patton eyed MacAuley closely. "What the hell were you doing in England? The war's over here, captain."

"Recuperating, sir," Mac answered.

"Captain MacAuley was wounded in France," a familiar voice behind him said. "He was a Jedburgh, working with the partisans behind German lines."

"Jedburghs. Partisans." Patton spat each word. "Damn way to fight a war, skulking around in the dark." To someone behind Mac, Patton added, "I guess that's what you OSS people do best."

"Yes, general, and it's important work," the voice answered. "It was Churchill who gave the order to set Europe ablaze."

"Of course, of course." Patton waved the fact away with his stick. "Got to keep the goddam Limeys happy," he muttered. "At least that's what Ike keeps telling me." As an afterthought, he added, "At ease, captain, at ease."

Mac relaxed, turned toward the unknown voice, and found Colonel Marcus Fender, head of OSS activities in Northern Europe, smiling at him.

"Hello, Mac," the colonel said. He was tall, though shorter than the general, and middle-aged, with dark hair turning gray. Deep creases lined his handsome face, far more than MacAuley remembered him having, but his upper lip still sported a pencil-thin Boston Blackie moustache. On his left jacket shoulder, he wore a different OSS patch, this one in the shape of a spearhead.

"Good to see you, colonel," Mac said.

Fender gripped Mac's shoulder as he shook his hand. "Good to see *you* up and around, Mac." Fender studied MacAuley's face. "Everything okay?"

"The leg's a hundred percent," Mac said, slapping his right thigh, "thanks to all that torture the medicos call 'physical therapy.' I was almost ready to tell them all the secrets I know."

Fender's stare didn't waiver. "I mean everything, Mac. You know … Vercors."

MacAuley's eyes squeezed tight, as if the word caused him physical pain. They opened again as he nodded. "Yes, sir, everything's fine."

"Good," Fender said, patting Mac's shoulder. "Let me introduce you to the others."

Mac took his first glance around the room. A young first lieutenant sat in a chair watching them. He had sand-colored hair, and a good-looking face with sharp features. Keen blue eyes studied Fender and MacAuley. He, too, wore an OSS spearhead patch. Another man stood behind Patton, studying a wall map.

Fender beckoned the lieutenant over. He was as tall as Mac but looked too thin for his height. He stared curiously at MacAuley as they shook hands.

"This is Lieutenant Harry Herschel," Fender said. "Harry's with X-2."

"OSS counter-intelligence?" Mac said.

"Yes, sir," Herschel said. "Though lately I've been seconded to Army counter-intelligence as an interrogator."

"Harry's a native German speaker," Fender said.

Mac eyed the lieutenant. "You're German?"

"Half," Heschel said. "My mother was German. My father was American. He was a historian teaching at the University of Frankfurt when they met after the last war. I was raised in the U.S., but my mother insisted I learn her tongue. And I studied at the Frankfurt university before this war."

"And I think you know that bum." Fender winked and nodded at the man studying the wall map.

The man at the map wore an enlisted man's uniform with staff-sergeant stripes, and the SF wings on his shoulder. He was medium height with a dark face and curly black hair that tickled his ears. As he turned from the map, he grinned at MacAuley.

"Hello. Mac."

Mac returned the grin and stepped forward, his hand stretched out. "Roy! You son-of-a-bitch!"

They clasped hands and patted each other's shoulder.

"That's no damn way for an enlisted man to greet a superior officer," Patton growled in his shrill voice.

The sergeant stood at attention and smartly saluted Mac, still grinning. "I mean, hello, sir, Captain MacAuley, sir!"

Mac returned the salute, then turned to Patton.

"Excuse us, general, Roy—um, Staff Sergeant Damper—was my radioman in France until he got wounded." He turned back to Damper. "Everything heal all right?"

Damper patted his stomach. "Everything's where it's supposed to be," he said. "Just a little less of it."

"Still no reason to discard common military courtesy," the general huffed.

"Our three-man Jedburgh teams dispense with military ranks when working behind enemy lines, general," Fender said.

"We think it's best not to reveal our rank even to the partisans we work with," Mac added, "in case one gets captured and tortured. The less they know about us, the less they can tell the krauts."

Mac noticed Herschel stiffen at the word "kraut."

"Well, colonel, they're not behind enemy lines now," Patton said. "They're behind *our* lines."

"Yes, sir," Fender said. "It won't happen again."

"See that it doesn't." The general walked behind his desk and sat. "Now let's get on with this damn briefing."

"Yes, sir." Fender opened a briefcase and removed some photos. "Gentlemen, please sit."

As Mac and Roy took chairs, Fender handed them the photos. They showed an arrow-shaped object, pointed at one end with what looked like fins at the other. Damper squinted at the photo, turned it one way, then the next, then held it out at arm's length.

"Is this one of those V-rockets the krauts have been hammering London with?" he asked.

Once again, Mac saw Herschel tense.

Fender chuckled and glanced at the photos. "Well, I guess it does look a little like a rocket, but no, sergeant."

"It's a knife of some kind, isn't it?" Mac said.

"Getting closer, Mac," Fender said. "It's a spear. Actually, it's the blade of a spear. You've probably heard of it. It's called the Spear of Destiny."

Roy frowned and shook his head. Mac thought for a moment and nodded.

"Something from the Crucifixion," he said. "It was used to stab Jesus on the cross."

"Correct," Fender said.

MacAuley shrugged and laid the photo down. "What about it?"

"Hitler has it; we want it," Fender said. "That's your next mission."

Chapter 4

"I'LL LET LIEUTENANT HERSCHEL provide you some background on the Spear of Destiny," Fender said. "He's our resident expert. Lieutenant."

Herschel stood, nodded to Fender, and said, "Sir, thank you." He turned to Patton and gestured to a wooden box on his desk. "General, with your permission." Patton nodded.

The lieutenant opened the box and withdrew what looked like the same object shown in the photographs. It was a foot-and-a-half long and about four inches at its widest. At the base was a two-inch wide receptacle for the pole that once served as its handle. The blade was dark gray except for a sheath of gold wrapped around its center. A crack ran lengthwise from the base and jammed inside the crack was some sort of spike. Intervals of tightly wound wire bound the spike and blade together.

"This is a replica of the Spear of Destiny," Herschel began. "Also known as the True Spear, the Holy Lance, and the Lance of Longinus." He handed MacAuley the replica spear.

"Oh, wait, I remember that name from Sunday school," Damper said. "The Roman soldier who gutted Christ."

"Yes, but he hardly 'gutted' Christ," Herschel said. "Longinus was a centurion with poor eyesight. He was ordered to determine whether Jesus was dead and used his spear to stab Jesus in the side. Jesus *was* already dead, but legend says blood and water dripped from the wound into Longinus's eyes, restoring his eyesight. Longinus then became an early convert to Christianity. He was eventually made a saint."

"Lieutenant, what does this writing say?" asked Mac, pointing to words stamped into the gold sheath.

"That is Latin for 'The Lance and Nail of our Lord'," the lieutenant said.

"And this spike inserted in the crack?" Again Mac.

"That is believed to be a nail from the cross," Herschel said. "Well, I mean on the real spear." He took the replica from MacAuley and held it up. "Originally, the blade wasn't this ornate. It was just an ordinary Roman spearhead. Constantine the Great—"

"Who?" asked Damper.

"Emperor Constantine of Rome," Mac said.

"The first *Christian* emperor of Rome," Herschel added. "After his conversion, he believed in the spear's power and carried it with him into battle. At some point, he gained the nail said to be from the cross and ordered the spear blade hollowed out and the nail inserted. Somehow during that process, the blade cracked, so they simply inserted the nail into the crack and bound the two together with wire. The gold sheath came later, as did a silver sheath beneath it and the decorative wings at its base."

MacAuley leaned back in his chair. "Thank you for your history lesson, lieutenant," he said. "Very interesting. But what does it have to do with the OSS?"

Herschel started to answer, but Patton slammed his hand on his desktop and launched from his chair. "Damn it, man, it's the Spear of Destiny. The Spear of *Destiny*!" He emphasized the last word.

"I'm sure the captain isn't familiar with the legend of the spear, general," Fender said calmly. Fender, as Mac knew, was legendary for his ability to remain calm when all hell was breaking loose. Captured early in the first war, Fender escaped from five German prisoner of war camps. He was recaptured each time, but with such aplomb his captors celebrated each attempt with him by sharing a bottle of cognac.

"Legend, hell!" Patton sputtered. "The Spear of Destiny!"

"Yes, but perhaps we could let the lieutenant continue?" the colonel asked.

Patton sat and waved his crop in the air. "Yes, yes. Go on, dammit."

The general's nasally whine grated on MacAuley's ears, and he wondered if Patton's well-known use of profanity was to compensate for his voice.

"Lieutenant, please continue," Fender said.

"Yes, sir," Herschel said. He pulled a notebook from his inside breast pocket, flipped it open, cleared his throat and began. "As I said, Constantine was the first Roman emperor to carry the spear into battle, but he wasn't the last. It passed from emperor to emperor. The Visigoth leader Alaric acquired it briefly when he sacked Rome in the 5th century, but he left it behind on his march to the north and died shortly after. Attila the Hun then received the spear as part of a ransom paid for not sacking Rome in 451. Before marching his army northward, the following year, Attila is said to have ridden his horse to the gates of Rome and tossed the spear at the feet of its defenders, saying, 'Take back your Holy Lance. It is of no use to me, since I do not know Him that made it holy.' Attila died a year later."

Herschel looked up from his notebook, hoping he hadn't put his audience to sleep and was happy to see all four of them were still wide awake. Patton, in fact, leaned forward on his desk, apparently enthralled at the lieutenant's lecture.

"With the return of the lance to Rome, it continued to be passed between emperors until the fall of the Western Roman Empire in 476. With the rise of the Holy Roman Empire in Europe in 800, the spear became part of the Imperial

Regalia—that is, the insignia of the office of the Roman emperor, which also includes his crown, robe, sword, cross, and other items that together we today call the Holy Roman Relics.

"Holy Roman emperors continued carrying the spear into battle. Charlemagne the Great, for instance, carried the spear during forty-seven victorious battles until he died after dropping it. The Holy Roman Empire grew to dominate most of Europe until the 1700s when its dominance dwindled to mostly the Germanic countries. The empire dissolved in 1806 after its defeat at the hands of Napoleon Bonaparte."

"For god's sake, lieutenant," growled Patton, "get to the important part."

"You mean the legend, sir?" Herschel asked.

"Yes, yes, dammit, go on," the general snapped.

"By the age of Napoleon, the lance had acquired its name, the Spear of Destiny, based on its legend that whoever possessed the spear would become a great conqueror. But if the spear were lost, the conqueror would lose either his power or his life—or both."

"This is based on what you told us about Charlemagne and Attila," Mac said.

"Yes, sir, and others throughout history," the lieutenant said. "Besides Charlemagne, there was the Byzantine emperor Justinian, Karl Martel of the Carolingian Dynasty,

Otto the Great, and more—all great men who rose to power while possessing the spear. Holy Roman Emperor Frederick Barbarossa I carried it during his campaigns against Italy and Turkey. He apparently dropped the spear while crossing the Saleph River and drowned minutes later.

"Napoleon was enamored with the spear and tried to seize it after the Battle of Austerlitz. The spear, along with the Imperial Regalia, then resided in Nuremburg. But fearing Napoleon would use the spear to rule over Europe, the Holy Relics were smuggled into Austria and placed into the custody of Baron von Hügel for safekeeping.

"However, the baron was less than scrupulous, and sold the relics—including the spear—to what remained of the Habsburg Dynasty. It is said that Kaiser Wilhelm II of Germany possessed the spear early in the century before it was returned to Vienna—"

"And he lost the last war and his empire!" Patton exclaimed.

"Yes, sir, he did," Herschel said before continuing. "After that, the relics were on display in the Hofburg Treasure House in Vienna, where a young Adolf Hitler became enthralled with the spear. In his book *Mein Kampf*, Hitler wrote—" Herschel flipped a page in his notebook. "'I felt as though I myself had held it in my hands before in some earlier century of history—that I myself had once claimed it as my talisman of power and held the destiny of the world in my hands'."

"And now Hitler has the spear," Mac said. "How did that happen?"

"He basically stole it from the Treasure House after the Anschluss in Thirty-eight," Herschel said. "It was taken back to Nuremburg, where it was put on public display. I saw it there myself when I was studying at the university before the war. When the Allies started bombing Germany, the spear and the relics were taken away and hidden. They haven't been seen since."

Mac scratched his head, then remembering Patton's demand for tidiness, smoothed his hair out. He turned to Fender. "Colonel, you said the Allies want the spear."

Fender nodded. "That is correct, Mac."

"And I am assuming that you want the sergeant here and me to retrieve it," MacAuley said. "I mean, that's why you called us here. Am I right?"

"You are," Fender said.

"Well …" Mac stretched out the word while rubbing his left check. "How are we supposed to retrieve it if no one knows where it is?"

Fender had the smile of a movie star, and he flashed it.

"Because Lieutenant Herschel thinks he knows where it's hidden," the colonel said.

Chapter 5

"THINKS?" MAC REPEATED.

"The lieutenant has developed some intelligence that we believe will lead us to the spear," Fender said. He turned to Herschel. "Harry, why don't you explain?"

Herschel cleared his throat again. "As I mentioned earlier, I've been on attached duty to army counter-intelligence, conducting interrogations of German POWs. With the war almost over, the number of POWs has swamped their own interrogation staff and ..."

"Goddammit, lieutenant," Patton growled. "We don't need a situation report on the status of the war. Move on!"

Herschel's face flushed as he stammered, "Ye—yes, sir." He cleared his throat again. "I was interviewing a POW—"

"Interviewing?" Patton again. "That's how you get information from the krauts? *Interviewing* them? Why don't you just ask them to fill out a survey?"

"We're not the Gestapo, general," Herschel said. "Even the Germans know the Gestapo's methods don't develop any good intelligence."

"Hell of a war we're fighting," Patton muttered, waving his riding crop again to signal Herschel to continue.

"I had been working with a prisoner named Steinbrink," Herschel said. "Not a young man. He was a retread from the last war and was not happy about being drafted for this one. I never got the feeling he had any valuable intelligence. He was a corporal and had only been in the lines a few weeks before he was captured. But he was from Nuremburg, and I hoped I might get some information on the city defenses that might be useful in our coming offensive there.

"I was about to release him for processing to a POW camp when, one day, he asked if I had ever heard of the Spear of Destiny. I told him I had seen it when I was a student. Then he asked me if I would like to know where it was hidden."

"How would a corporal have that kind of information?" Mac asked.

"As I said, he was from Nuremburg," Herschel said. "Grew up there. His parents own a bakery. He told me when the Allies started bombing German cities, the Nazis built an underground bunker to hide the Roman relics and other art treasures in the city. And they built it with the entrance hidden in a parking garage directly under the Steinbrink's bakery. They used to provide baked goods to the guards posted in the bunker."

"Nuremburg's a big city, lieutenant," MacAuley said. "There must be hundreds of bakeries there. How do we know which one?"

"Steinbrink drew me a map," Herschel said.

"How do we know the map is accurate?" Mac said. "He could have drawn you a map of Heidelberg."

"It was pretty easy to vet, captain," Harry said. "The Steinbrink bakery is located in an area called Blacksmith's Alley, right across the street from Nuremberg Castle."

"We had the map verified, Mac," Fender interjected. "Once Lieutenant Herschel developed this information, he wrote a report and sent it and a copy of the map up the chain of command. It caused quite a stir, I can tell you."

"It damn sure did," Patton added.

"We had Corporal Steinbrink's hand-drawn map superimposed over recent aerial reconnaissance photos of Nuremburg," Fender said. "We were able to verify the streets and the location of the bunker." He nodded to Herschel. "Lieutenant, please continue."

"The Steinbrink bakery sits atop a parking garage across from the castle," Herschel said. "According to Steinbrink, the Germans built the bunker entrance below the bakery with a ramp leading from the garage into the bunker. The entrance is sealed by a steel door. Apparently, the Nazis built it in great secrecy. The only reason the Steinbrinks know about it is because the construction took place under their very feet and, as I mentioned, they provide the guards with baked goods. But the Gestapo warned them never to talk about it."

"Excuse me, lieutenant," Roy Damper said, scratching his ear. "But I think Mac—um, Captain MacAuley—and I are on the same wavelength on this. Why would Steinbrink just give you this information? What's he get in return?"

"Corporal Steinbrink wants to emigrate to the States when the war is over," Herschel answered. "He said he was tired of Germany's wars. I agreed to help him when the time came."

"*Can* you help him?" MacAuley asked.

"It will be in his POW record he was cooperative," Harry said. "And that he wasn't a hard-core Nazi."

Mac stood and stepped to the large wall map. "Okay, so this Spear of Destiny is in a bunker in Nuremburg," he said. "But even a cursory look at this map shows Nuremburg is still in kraut hands."

"Seventh Army is targeting it as soon as they capture Aschaffenburg," Fender said.

Mac had an empty feeling in his gut. He didn't like what he was hearing.

"So, we wait until the Seventh captures Nuremberg, then go fetch the spear?" asked Roy. He glanced at Mac, and MacAuley could tell Roy didn't like the direction the conversation was going either.

"Wait, hell!" roared Patton. "We wait for the krauts to retreat, they'll take the goddam spear with them!"

"The general's right, Mac," Fender added. "If we wait for the city to be evacuated, the Germans are likely to move the Holy Relics—"

"The spear, colonel," Patton griped. "The *spear*."

"Including the spear," Fender said. "We can't let that happen."

"Because of this legend Lieutenant Herschel told us about?" Mac said. Patton and Fender both nodded.

"Exactly!" Patton rose from his chair, his riding crop held high like a sword. "With the Spear of Destiny, I—we, that is—America could wipe the commie scourge right off the face of Mother Earth."

As one, the four other men in the room glanced uncomfortably at each other. Patton noted their discomfort and lowered his riding crop, clearing his throat. "Of course, Ike would probably want to return the spear—" He waved his crop as if pointing at something. "—back to Austria where it belongs." He cleared his throat. "Gentleman, if you'll excuse me. I have an inspection tour to conduct."

Patton picked up his glistening, lacquered helmet emblazed with four stars. The others snapped to attention as he tapped his forehead with the riding crop and left the room. As the door closed, each man let out an audible sigh. Then Fender continued.

"Going back to your original question—no, Mac, we're not waiting until Nuremberg is in our hands. General

Patch's Seventh Army hasn't reached Aschaffenburg yet. Once we take Aschaffenburg, Nuremberg will lay open to our advance."

Mac's stomach churned, and his mouth turned dry. "And since you don't want to wait that long," he concluded, "you want Roy and me to sneak into Nuremberg, enter that bunker, and steal the spear."

"You, Roy, *and* Lieutenant Herschel," Fender said.

Now bile surged up Mac's throat. "You want—him? You want me to take him?" He jabbed a finger at Herschel. "No offense, lieutenant. I'm sure you're a swell interrogator, but you don't have any experience behind the lines."

"Neither did you the first time, Mac," Fender said gently. "It was Major Summersby of the British SOE who led your first mission, I believe."

"He's got you there, Mac," Roy said. With Patton gone, he relapsed into his old familiarity.

"Captain, I have much of the same training as you," Herschel said. "Camp X and all of it. And while I have no experience as a Jedburgh behind German lines, I *lived* in Nuremberg. I know the city and its people. And, as the colonel pointed out earlier, I speak German like a native. And, more than that, sir, it's your mission. You're in charge. But you *do* need me."

"What do you mean I need you?" Mac looked at Fender. "What's he mean by that?"

"Lieutenant Herschel is the only person who can verify the identity of the spear," Fender said. "His father, the late Dr. Henry Herschel, and his research partner, the late Professor Franz Bollag, discovered how to identify the True Spear while working for the Hofburg Museum in Vienna in the Thirties. Note, I said the 'late Dr. Henry Herschel' and 'the late Professor Franz Bollag,' Mac. Dr. Herschel shared that secret with only one person while on his deathbed, and that was his son. So, you see, you need *him* to make the identification."

Chapter 6

"AND HE CAN'T JUST tell me how to identify it?"

"No, Mac," Fender said. "Dr. Herschel and his colleague swore to keep the secret of how to identify it to themselves."

"If their method of identifying the spear became publicly known," added Herschel, "there would be a plethora of fake spears flooding the antiquities market—all appearing to be the one True Spear."

"That would be bad?" Mac asked.

"That would be bad, captain," Harry answered.

Mac frowned and sighed, did a half turn, scratched his ear, then turned back.

"Fine. All right," he said. "You're with us." He turned to Colonel Fender. "How are we supposed to pull off this heist? I assume you already have a plan?"

Fender flashed his movie-star smile and nodded. He stepped up to the wall map and pointed to a spot a few miles outside Nuremberg. "You three will be flown here by a Lysander, the same one that flew you, Mac, in from London. It's still waiting for you at the airstrip. Your cover will be a lieutenant colonel in the SS SD. You've played that role before and your cover identity, from all we can tell, is still valid."

"I hope so," Mac muttered.

"Lieutenant Herschel will be your aide, and Roy will be your driver."

"Excuse me, colonel," Roy said. "My French is fluent, but my German is just so-so."

"That's why your cover will be a sergeant in SS Charlamagne Division, a pro-Nazi French volunteer wounded on the Eastern Front and seconded to the SD for light duty."

"What about uniforms and weapons?" Mac asked. "Do you have a supply here?"

Fender nodded. "Uniforms and papers, as well as weapons, have been prepared for you and flew in with you on the same plane."

Realization struck Mac. "You assumed we'd agree to this idiocy?" he growled.

Fender sighed. "Mac, be realistic. You never had a choice. None of you did. Patton wants the spear—bad."

"Yeah, about Patton," Mac said. "Nuremberg is in Seventh Army's operational area. Patton only commands Third Army. Isn't he encroaching on Patch's rice bowl?"

"OSS is a theater asset, Mac," Fender said. "Patton wants the spear, but Eisenhower wants to recover *all* the Holy Relics. You're operating under Ike's orders. Understood?"

Mac sighed. "Understood."

"Now, we have agents already positioned near your landing site," Fender continued. "They'll meet you at the plane and take you to a safe house. Recognition signals have been arranged and will be provided to you before you board the Lysander. Our agents will provide you with transportation, a Kübelwagen. You'll take this road here straight into the eastern part of the city—away from the western defenses being prepared. Harry has a map of the city, and you three can decide the best approach to the bunker."

"Excuse me, colonel," Roy said, "you said General Eisenhower wants *all* the relics. How many relics are there and how big are they? Those German jeeps aren't much bigger than ours."

"Good question, Roy," Fender said. "And I'm glad you asked it because the solution rests with you."

"Not sure I'm going to like this," Roy whispered to Mac.

"Your mission is to bring back only the spear," Fender said. "The Monuments Men will recover the rest of the relics—"

"The what?" MacAuley asked.

"The Monuments, Fine Arts, and Archives section of military civil affairs," Harry said. "Art historians, museum curators, and such who are scouring all the former German-occupied territories for art looted by the Germans. Their nickname is the Monuments Men."

"Sounds like this mission is more in line with their work," Mac said.

"It will be," Fender said, "once Nuremberg is captured. And ensuring the relics stay in the bunker until the Monuments Men get there is going to be your job, Roy." Fender turned to look at Damper. "Once you snatch the spear, Roy will blow up the entrance to the bunker so nothing more can be taken from it."

"I knew I wouldn't like it," Roy mumbled.

"And once we have the spear, how do we get back?" Mac asked.

"Retrace your steps back to the safe house," Fender said. "Our agents will notify us by radio, and the Lysander will pick you up." The colonel collected the photographs he distributed earlier and jammed them into his briefcase. "The codename for this mission is Parsifal."

"Parsifal? Isn't that German for Perceval, King Arthur's knight who went in search of the Holy Grail?"

"Yes and no," Harry said. "Parsifal is from the Wagnerian opera. Basically, the same story, but before Parsifal can go in search of the Grail, he first has to find the Spear of Destiny and return it to his king."

Fender looked at each of the three men. "Any more questions?" They each shook their head.

"Just a snatch-and-grab, colonel," Roy said. "Should be a piece of cake."

He wasn't smiling when he said it.

☼

The young jeep driver was waiting for the three men outside the church as they left the meeting. As they careened through the rubble of the town, Mac turned from the front passenger seat to look back at Herschel and Damper.

"Lieutenant, do you believe this legend of the Spear of Destiny?"

Herschel scratched his chin and considered what to answer. "I'm not a particularly religious man, captain. I'm a historian by training. As such, I consider the Holy Roman Relics to be invaluable historical objects. But sometimes an object—a talisman like the spear—while not holding any intrinsic mystical powers itself can be endowed with mystical power simply by the belief that people put into it."

"Like a lucky rabbit's foot," offered Roy.

"Like a lucky rabbit's foot," Herschel agreed. "Or a crucifix. Or any number of treasured or worshipped objects in the world. Many Germans are heavily into mysticism. Much of the Nazi rhetoric takes advantage of that. The so-called 'blood flag' from Hitler's failed putsch and stained with the blood of what the Nazis call martyrs is used to sanctify other Nazi flags. The swastika itself is a talisman of sorts. It's been used by different religions all over the world. So,

41

something like the Spear of Destiny may gain its powers just because people *believe* in its power."

"And Hitler believes in its power?" Mac said.

"You heard what he wrote," Harry said. He paused, biting his lower lips as he considered the rest of his answer. "But I don't believe Hitler is much into religion or mysticism. Not as much as Heinrich Himmler. Himmler formed the entire SS around mystical beliefs like the Teutonic Knights. He's a devotee of the German mystic Guido von List, considered by many to be the father of Aryan mythology. The lightning bolts worn on SS uniforms are based on the Armanen runes created by List.

"And Himmler is a deep believer in the Spear of Destiny. I read he keeps a replica of the spear on his desk at Wewelsburg Castle, the holy shrine of the SS. Years before the war, Himmler gave another spear replica to Hitler with the promise that the actual spear would soon be in Hitler's possession, and he delivered on that promise after the Anschluss."

"So, you're saying the spear itself isn't powerful," Mac summed up. "It's that people simply believe it has powers."

"Yes, sir. Have you heard of the placebo effect?"

Mac nodded. "That's when a doctor gives something like a sugar pill to a patient, and the patient starts feeling better, right?"

Harry nodded. "Usually given to people who are hypochondriacs," he said. "They *believe* they're sick and manifest the symptoms of an illness. When the doctor gives them a sugar pill, they *believe* it's a cure and the symptoms of the illness disappear."

"Mind over matter," said Roy.

"In a manner of speaking, yes," Harry said. "You know, Himmler's not the only one who believes in the legend of the spear. You heard what General Patton said. He believes in the spear, too."

"That's not the only thing he believes in," Mac said. "He thinks he's been reincarnated. He says he's fought battles in the distant past over the same fields we've been fighting over."

"I've read that in the newspapers," Harry said. "What's that tell you about him?"

Mac shook his head. "You tell me."

"That there's a very fine dividing line," Harry said, "between brilliance and insanity."

Chapter 7

THAT NIGHT, THE PARSIFAL team went over their plans. A Jedburgh team organizing Romani resistance fighters in the German rear areas would meet them at the landing site. Romani lineage reached back to immigrants from India and, as such, were considered racially inferior by the Nazis and, like Jews, were rounded up and sent to labor and death camps. A few who escaped capture formed resistance groups.

The Jedburghs would take the Parsifal team to their safe house and brief them on what a Romani reconnaissance of Nuremberg had discovered about the location of the underground bunker. Mac always believed the simplest plans were the best. He wanted simply to drive up to the bunker's hidden entrance in the Kübelwagen and demand entry. Brazen, certainly, but he felt his rank as an SS obersturmbannführer was enough to intimidate any guards.

"It's almost a certainty the guard detail will be small," Mac explained to Roy and Harry. "The krauts in Nuremberg know the Allies are coming for them. They'll have every available soldier manning the defenses. No more than a lieutenant would lead a small guard detail. With my rank and these papers—" Mac tapped an envelope holding orders signed with the forged signature of Heinrich Himmler. "I don't think there will be any trouble gaining entrance."

"Mac can be very intimidating as an SS colonel," Roy said. "Almost as if he were born to the role."

MacAuley scowled at Damper. "You just watch my back while I'm dealing with the guards. Don't strike up any conversations with anyone. Your German's not that good, even for a Charlemagne SS. And don't forget to limp. You're supposed to be convalescing."

Roy held up a roll of gauze bandage. "I'm going to wrap my left knee up with this," he said. "Should give me a good limp."

"What about me?" Harry asked.

"Just stay in the car," Mac said. "Don't do anything or say anything until I tell you to."

"Captain, Colonel Fender told you I speak German like a native—"

"Achtung, obersturmführer!" Mac shouted.

Roy Damper jumped to attention and extended his arm in the Nazi salute. Herschel glanced curiously at the radioman, then at MacAuley.

"Achtung, obersturmführer!" Mac repeated, glaring at Herschel. "Das meinst du!" *Attention, lieutenant! That means you!*

Herschel straightened to attention the way the American army trained him.

"Wenn ich linen Befehl gebe, erwarte ich, dass er aus-geführt und nicht diskutiert wird! Verstanden?" *When I give an order, I expect it to be carried out, not debated. Understood?*

"Jawohl," answered Harry.

"Jawohl, Herr Obersturmbannführer," Mac corrected.

"Jawohl, Herr Obersturmbannführer," Harry repeated.

"You don't only have to speak like a German," Mac said. "You have to act like a Nazi SS officer, think like a Nazi SS officer. And, for god's sake, stand at attention like a Nazi. Look at Roy."

Harry glanced at Damper, who was still standing rigid and motionless, his right arm still extended.

"Roy, work with him on that, will you?" Mac said. "I've got to talk to Fender."

"Jawohl, Herr Obersturmbannführer!"

Roy winked at Mac. MacAuley smirked, shook his head, and left.

Roy worked with Harry, coaching him on how an SS officer holds himself, presents himself, and how he should respond to those of lower rank and higher rank. Then he got an idea.

"Let's get our uniforms on," he said. "Maybe it'll help you get into character."

It worked. Once wearing the SS field gray, Herschel felt a change in the way he carried himself. Even though far less elaborate than the dreaded SS black dress uniform, the SS field uniform, with its lightning bolt runes, still exuded power and ruthlessness. He strutted into the planning room where Damper was already waiting and shouted, "Achtung!"

Roy snapped to attention, gave the Nazi salute, then grinned. "Better," he said. "Much better."

Harry swaggered around the room, his right thumb hooked over his Sam Brown belt, eyeing Roy as if inspecting him. He plucked at the tri-color piping on Roy's sleeve, identifying him as a French volunteer. "SS-Division Karls des Großen?" he said. "Sprechen sie Deutsch, Scharführer?" *SS Charlamagne Division? Do you speak German, staff sergeant?*

"Oui," Roy said, keeping in character. "Ich meine, ja, mein Herr. Aber nicht sehr viel oder gut." *I mean, yes, sir. But not very much or good.*

"I'll say," Herschel said. "Your accent and pronunciation are terrible."

"But my French is impeccable," Roy said. He kissed his fingertips and made a popping noise. "Magnifique!"

"Where'd you learn?" Harry said.

"Oh, I grew up speaking it," Roy said. "My father's American, but my mother was French Canadian. We lived in Quebec until my mother died, then my old man brought us back to the States."

"Mac's German is very good," Harry said. "Where did he learn it?"

"Oh, Mac's a regular linguist, that one," Roy said. "Studied Germanic languages at Oxford before the war. Spent his holidays in Germany and Scandinavia—when he wasn't chasing skirts in Paris. Speaks fluent German, Norwegian, and Swedish. And his French is more than passable. That's how he ended up in the OSS."

"Oh?"

"When he was at Oxford in 1940, before the U.S. entered the war, British intelligence approached him," Damper said. "Asked him to do some favors for them. As a neutral, he could still go places Brits couldn't—in both Germany and occupied France. When Wild Bill set up the OSS, British intelligence recommended Mac to him. Mac's been running operations since North Africa."

Wild Bill referred to Major General William "Wild Bill" Donovan, the WWI veteran and Medal of Honor recipient who established the OSS at the request of President Franklin D. Roosevelt.

"I have to admit, that sounds impressive," Harry said. He scratched his chin, contemplating what he was going to ask next. "He doesn't like me, does he?"

"Mac? It's not a matter of liking you, lieutenant—"

"Call me Harry," Herschel said. "That's what Mac told the general, right? You use first names."

Roy nodded. "It's not a matter of liking you, Harry," he said. "He just doesn't want to get to know you."

Harry puzzled over that, then asked, "Why?"

"You know anything about the Battle of Vercors?" Roy asked.

"Not much," Harry said, shaking his head. "A French resistance battle with the Germans."

Roy snorted. "More like the Alamo with a French attitude," he said. "The Vercors Massif is a giant plateau in southeastern France. The Maquis used it as a staging area for operations. Last summer, after the landings at Normandy, the Allied brass got the smart idea of having the various bands of resistance groups come together at Vercors to form a sort of resistance army. The idea was to draw German forces away from the Normandy front and the landing beaches for Operation Dragoon, the invasion of southern France. Ten of us—half OSS, half SOE—jumped into Vercors to train them how to fight like regular army soldiers. We were promised reinforcement with airborne troops and supply drops of artillery, bazookas—you name it. All we had to do was keep the krauts occupied for a couple of weeks until the Dragoon landings took place."

Roy sat at a table and stared for a moment at the far wall, remembering. "Well, Dragoon got delayed for two months.

We got one large supply drop—in the middle of the day! Can you believe that? The Luftwaffe was still flying in eastern France, and they bombed the hell out of the drop zone and gunned down anyone who tried to get to the supply cannisters. After that, all we got were a few night supply drops, not enough to equip an army. And the only airborne troops to land at Vercors were German. It was a rout, a goddamn rout!" Roy emphasized the last sentence by slamming his fist on the table. "One of the last wireless transmissions from the Maquis said …" Roy paused to recall the quote correctly. "'We shall not forget the bitterness of having been abandoned alone and without support in time of battle.'"

He took a deep breath and sighed.

"I got wounded pretty early on and flown out by Lysander," he continued. "Mac was hit shortly before the end. Some of the surviving Maquis got him off the massif and hid him until the Dragoon landings took place a month later and the Allies liberated the area. By the time Mac got back to London, he was determined someone would pay for the slaughter. He demanded an investigation, threatened to write Congress for hearings, all that kind of stuff. Meanwhile, the brass just kind of shoveled what happened at Vercors under the carpet."

"I overheard Colonel Fender ask Mac if he was okay now about Vercors," Harry said. "I guess he got over it."

"What makes you think that?" Roy asked. "Look, the war's almost over. If I know Mac, once it's finished, he'll get his revenge."

Herschel thought about what Roy told him. "It still doesn't answer my original question, Roy. Why doesn't Mac want to get to know me, like you said?"

Roy took out a pack of cigarettes and lit one. "Want one? They're German."

Harry took one and let Roy light it from an old German trench lighter. "By the way, if you have any American or British smokes on you—matches, lighter, anything—get rid of them. You can smoke German, French, or Russian ciga- rettes—any kind a kraut might pick up from one of the oc- cupied areas and that's it."

Herschel drew a pack from his tunic and tossed it on the table along with a box of matches from a K-ration box. "Thanks, good advice," he said. "But you're avoiding the question."

Damper blew some smoke rings, then said, "No, I'm not. I'm considering how to answer it." He took another deep drag and let the smoke trail from his nose. "I told you ten of us jumped into Vercors to train the Maquis, right?"

"Yes."

"Mac and I are the only survivors," Roy said. "The rest were killed or captured—which is basically the same thing, just slower and more painful. We learned later many were slaughtered after an SS major talked them into surrendering. Said they'd be treated honorably as soldiers and prisoners of war. He got them to lay down their weapons and muster in a field where he addressed them. He sneezed and took out a handkerchief as if to wipe his nose but dropped it. That was his signal for hidden machine guns to open up on the Maquis. All of them were killed. Some of them Mac had known for a long time, including Major Summersby of the SOE. He was sort of Mac's mentor and close friend."

"Fender mentioned him, right?" Harry said. "Led Mac's first mission."

Roy nodded and squashed out his cigarette. "This close to the end of the war, Mac doesn't want to lose any more friends," he said. "And that means not making any more friends."

Chapter 8

"I DON'T LIKE IT."

"Like what?" Fender said as MacAuley entered his quarters.

"Herschel," Mac said. "He's inexperienced." He took out a cigarette and lit it. "It's too late in the war to bring newcomers up to speed. He's an encumbrance."

"He's the only person who knows how to identify the True Spear," Fender said.

"You said that already."

"That fact hasn't changed since this afternoon," Fender said. "You need him."

"You said that, too," Mac replied.

Fender nodded as he lit his own cigarette. "And that fact hasn't changed either."

"I don't trust him," Mac said.

Fender exhaled a lungful of smoke and gave Mac a look that made him feel like a school child in the principal's office. "Why not?"

"Didn't you notice how he cringed when we called the Jerries 'krauts'?" Mac said.

"Yes, I did. So?"

"If he gets upset at people calling Jerries krauts …" Mac let the sentence die, realizing what he might sound like.

"Then maybe he's a sympathizer?" Fender asked.

"You said it, not me." Mac snubbed out his cigarette and lit another.

"Perhaps even a spy?"

"He did spend a lot of time in Germany before the war," Mac said. "Even after the Nazis came to power."

"So did you, Mac."

"That was different," Mac protested. "I was working for the Brits—unofficially."

"You spent a lot of time in Germany before MI6 approached you," Fender reminded him. He reached into a desk drawer and removed a bottle of scotch. He pointed to a small coffee service across the room. "Fetch a couple of those cups."

Mac brought the ceramic cups over and Fender poured each a healthy measure.

Fender took a sip from his cup and smacked his lips. "Before the war, I was strictly a bourbon man," he said. "With all the time I spent in England, I've developed a real taste for this stuff." He took another drink. "You don't really think Herschel's a German spy now, do you, Mac?"

"It's been known to happen." Mac drank from his cup, frowned, then shook his head. "He's too inexperienced. He's not trained for the field. He's an interrogator, for

Christ's sake. He's liable to get himself killed—and me and Roy with him."

Fender nodded. "Inexperienced in the field, yes," he said. "But not untrained for it."

Mac waited for the colonel to explain.

"Harry was trained for a Jedburgh mission," Fender said. "And he excelled at the training. He was a natural at it. He was set to drop into France along with a British officer from SOE and a Free French lieutenant. A day before he was to leave, he got pulled from the mission."

Mac's eyes narrowed. "Pulled? Why?"

"Someone upstairs determined agents with family members living in Germany were too susceptible to blackmail if they were captured," Fender said. "The Gestapo could threaten to harm their family members to get them to talk or agree to work as double agents."

Mac shrugged and nodded. "I can see that."

"We offered Harry a position on a Jedburgh mission to China," Fender said. "But he said he wanted to fight Nazis. He didn't like what he saw in Germany after Hitler came to power any more than you did. So, with his German fluency, we put him in X-2 as an interrogator. And he's a damn good interrogator, Mac. He has a way of getting prisoners and suspects to talk to him. That Steinbrink info wasn't the first piece of good intel he developed."

Mac finished off his drink. "I see," he said. "But he could still get captured on this job. Even with the war almost over, the krauts could still use family members in Germany to blackmail him. Did you think of that?"

Fender waved away Mac's concern. "That's not a problem anymore, Mac," he said. "We don't think any of them are still alive. They were all sent to the camps." Fender leveled his gaze at MacAuley. "Harry's a Jew, Mac. That's why he wants to fight Nazis."

The door to Fender's quarters burst open, and a German NCO dashed through wielding a Schmeisser MP-40 machine pistol. Behind him strutted a German officer holding a Walther P-38 pistol.

"Stehen Sie, wo Sie sind! Bewege dich nicht und du wirst leben!" said the officer. *Stand where you are! Do not move and you will live!*

☼

Instinct made Mac's hand go straight for the .45 automatic on his hip, but common sense made him freeze. The German officer paraded around the room, regarding Mac with the same look he might have had if he'd stepped on dog droppings. Then he grinned.

Mac shook his head. "You idiots. You could have gotten yourselves shot."

"Nah, Mac," Roy Damper said. "We had the drop on you. Is that scotch I see?"

"All right," Mac said. "You did good, Roy. You're a natural teacher. Colonel?"

Fender nodded and Mac fetched two more cups from the coffee service. The colonel divvied out more of the scotch and raised his cup in a salute. "To our captors."

Roy and Harry clicked their heels and bowed, then drank their whiskey.

"You know what they say about the clothing making the man," Roy said. "It's true. As soon as Harry—he insists I call him that, by the way—as soon as Harry put on that uniform, he became a regular Conrad Veidt."

"It is an impressive uniform," Herschel said. "If our army had uniforms like this, I might stay in after the war." He chuckled at his own joke. "Seriously, it was what you told me, captain—"

"Mac," MacAuley said.

"Mac." Harry clicked his heels as if still in character. "It was what you said about thinking and acting like a Nazi officer. God knows I saw enough of them when I was at the university. I just started remembering what I thought about them—especially the SS louts. Everything I hated about them I put into my character."

"A regular method actor," Fender said, grinning like a screen idol.

"So, Herr Obersturmbannführer," Harry said, "when do we leave?"

"Don't be so anxious," Mac said. "We still have some planning to do, and you still need to get used to being an SS officer."

"No time for that, Mac," Fender said, his grin gone. "I was going to tell you earlier, but we got distracted by ... *your request*. You're going out tomorrow night. The rendezvous with our team outside Nuremberg has been arranged. We need to get you in and out of the city before General Patch starts his assault. From the intel we've got about the city's defenses, it's going to be a slaughterhouse for both sides."

Chapter 9

THE WESTLAND LYSANDER MK III SCW was an ungainly looking bird. Its short, rather stubby fuselage was topped by equally stubby gull wings with trailing edges that canted forward as if they were installed backward. V-shaped struts supported the wings and its fixed landing gear sported bulbous wheel housings. A massive cockpit that looked like a greenhouse covered nearly half the upper fuselage. The blunt nose housed an air-cooled radial engine that turned a three-bladed prop. Adding to its inelegance was a fat exterior "belly tank" and a four-rung ladder that clung to its port side. In an age of aerodynamically streamlined thoroughbreds like the Spitfire and P-51 Mustang fighter planes, the Lysander looked like a sway-back old nag.

Yet the Lysander had qualities that set it apart from other aircraft. The awkward wings and oversized tailplane gave it an incredibly slow stall speed of only fifty-five miles per hour. That and the reinforced fixed landing gear allowed the Lysander to land and take off on short, unimproved fields, making it the perfect aircraft for the RAF Special Duty Service whose job it was to covertly deliver SOE and OSS agents and their supplies to German-occupied France.

Since those missions were flown only at night, the uninspiring Lysander wore an uninspiring coat of flat black paint.

"Come along then, lads," said the RAF pilot. He wore a flying suit topped by a heavy leather flight jacket with a wool collar turned up, and thick flying boots. His name was Flaherty. He didn't know the names of the Americans in German uniforms, except for Mac, whom he had flown in from England two days earlier. As for the others, they were merely "Joes," and he didn't need to know their names. "Let's not keep the war waiting. It'll be over soon enough, you know."

Harry started to climb the ladder to the rear cockpit, but Mac stopped him. "Roy and I will squeeze into the back," he said. "You take the window seat behind the pilot."

"But—"

"You won't get another chance to watch the fireworks if we take any ground fire," MacAuley explained. "It'll give you a whole new perspective on the Fourth of July."

Damper and Mac crawled into the tiny space behind the rear cockpit, followed by Harry, who took the rear seat.

"Right, then," Flaherty said. "Here we go, now."

The engine howled, and the Lysander stumbled down the airstrip and leapt into the air. Wind whipped through the open cockpit, kept opened so they could disembark immediately after landing. Within minutes, they were over the German lines and taking ground fire. Allied bombers had pummeled Nuremberg for weeks, and the German gunners were on high alert. Harry watched columns of tracers arcing through the air, ducking when any appeared to come near. Not that ducking would have helped if any of the tracers or the invisible bullets that accompanied them struck the plane. The thin metal and fabric skin of the aircraft offered no protection at all.

Herschel turned and shouted at MacAuley to be heard over the engine and the howl of the wind. "Thanks, Mac. You're right. I'll never watch a Fourth of July celebration the same way again."

Moments later, there was a crack and the plane shuddered. "What just happened?" Harry shouted to the pilot.

"Damn Jerries winged me plane," Flaherty answered, nodding to the starboard wing, which now had a large hole surrounded by flapping pieces of torn fabric. "Damn cheeky of them."

Harry stared at the damaged wing until he realized his hands and arms were aching from gripping his seat. "Can we still fly?"

"Don't be a silly dilly," Flaherty said. "Of course, we can still fly. See, we're still in the air. I'll have it patched once I get back to the airfield." Then, under his breath so Harry couldn't hear, he added, "Assuming the bloody wing doesn't fall off first."

The Lysander flew on, leaving the aerial spectacle of ground fire behind. A few minutes later, Flaherty turned and pointed to the ground in front of the plane. "There's our strip!"

Herschel sat up to look out the cockpit. Several miles ahead, he saw a single light blink the Morse Code letter M. Flaherty responded by flashing his landing lights just once, after which a series of small lights flared on the ground in the shape of an inverted L.

"Right then, here we go," the pilot said. "Tell your mates to prepare for landing."

The Lysander settled to the ground with a hard bump, and bounced past the landing lanterns until it reached the foot of the L and spun around. "Out!" shouted Flaherty.

Harry scrambled down the ladder, followed by Mac and Roy. As soon as the agents were out of the plane, it started rumbling down the improvised air strip and was soon back in the air. The three men crouched in the darkness as silent shadows darted from one lantern to the next, extinguishing them. Then a voice in the dark murmured, "Bist du das, Ernst?" *Is that you, Ernst?*

"Nein, ich bin es, Johann," Mac replied in a whisper. *No, it's me, Johann.*

A dark figure seemed to materialize next to them. "Captain MacAuley, I presume?"

"Here," Mac answered.

"Lieutenant Peters," the man said, pronouncing his rank as left-tenant. "SOE. Come with me."

They followed Peters through a stand of trees, where two men joined them. Romani fighters, Peters explained. They moved slowly to avoid stumbling over roots and rocks and to keep the sound of their movements as quiet as possible. After about an hour, they came to an abandoned farmhouse and stopped. Moonlight revealed deciduous fields and collapsed wooden fences. No light shone from the house.

One of the Romani moved forward toward the house, crouched, and softly called out a word in a language that none of the three Americans understood.

"Sinti Romani code word," Peters explained. "Jerry doesn't speak Sinti Romani. For that matter, neither do other Romani clans. Bloody complex thing, Romani."

A voice replied from the house and Peters grunted. "There's the counter word. Good show. Shall we go?"

The man on guard swung open the farmhouse door as they approached and closed it behind them. From all indications, the farmhouse hadn't been lived in for years. Layers of dust covered every surface. The glass in the windows was cracked or missing. Mold from years of rain leaking in grew on the walls.

"You'll have to pardon our housekeeping," Peters said with a slight smile. "The maid's been out ill."

The two Romani who had joined them in the trees rushed across the room, moved a pile of boxes, and opened a trap door. Peters climbed down a ladder, followed by the yanks. They landed in a small vestibule sealed off from the rest of the basement by a thick blanket hanging from a rope strung along the ceiling.

"This farm was owned by a Romani family," Peters said. "One of the few Romani families to settle down here in Germany. They were arrested and sent to the camps years ago. We try to keep the upstairs looking abandoned, so other than the guards on watch, we do everything down here."

Peters pulled back the blanket, revealing a roomy underground cavern lit by oil lamps. A table stood in the center, half covered by a map, the other half with food dishes and utensils. Empty crates standing on end served as stools. Cartons of ammunition, grenades, and other supplies stood stacked in one corner. Several weapons, including Mauser rifles, MP-40 machine pistols, and a panzerfaust antitank rocket, occupied another corner. The air reeked of human sweat mixed with smoke from the lamps and an untold number of cigarettes.

Two men sat at the table. "Lieutenants Sweeney and La Bou," Peters said. The two men nodded but didn't get up. "La Bou's Free French," Peters said. "For some bloody reason, he decided to stay with SOE after France was liberated."

La Bou pushed out his lower lip and shrugged. "But I love the wonderful working conditions."

La Bou noticed the French tricolor piping on Roy's uniform and his eyes narrowed. "Division SS Charlemagne?"

Roy replied in French, and La Bou straightened. He replied, also in French, and grinned at Roy's response. He stood and embraced Damper, then led him over to the table and gave him a box to sit on.

Peter smiled at Mac. "So, your boy's French Canadian, eh? Well, he made La Bou's day. He's the closest thing to a Frenchman La Bou's met in months."

Chapter 10

THEY WEREN'T WITH THE Jedburghs for long. Peters and his men supplied a map of Nuremberg and the surrounding area and showed them the best route to the city. They were briefed on what to expect as they drove toward Nuremberg—the locations and numbers of checkpoints—and what to expect once they entered the city.

"You say you've been to Nuremberg before?" Peters asked Harry.

"Yes, I studied at the university," Herschel answered.

"Well, brace yourself before you enter the city," Peters said. "The RAF pounded the bloody hell out of it back in January with blockbuster bombs and incendiaries, and there have been several more raids since then. They didn't only go after the weapons factories surrounding the city; they wanted to demolish what Adolf considers the heart of the Nazi Party."

"Nuremberg is where they held all those big party rallies," Mac said.

"Precisely," Peters said. "And they're not going to be holding any rallies there anytime soon."

When the briefing finished, there was just time enough for a couple of hours of sleep prior to setting off before dawn.

☼

The Kübelwagen, the German answer to the American jeep, hummed through the predawn dark, its blacked-out headlights emitting only thin slits of light. By the time they reached the main road to Nuremberg from the south, the dark had given way to the first strands of sunlight slipping over the eastern horizon. The road was busy with military traffic—trucks, tanks, artillery, and soldiers heading to defend the city from the American Seventh Army's pending assault. No one paid attention to another military vehicle joining the convoy. Nor did anyone protest when the Kübelwagen with two SS officers in the back seat—one of them a colonel—sped past them on the opposite side of the road.

The guards at the checkpoints gave only cursory glances at the three SS men as they approached. Most never asked for papers; the twin lightning bolts on the officers' collars were usually enough for the guards to wave them through. Only one guard demanded to see their identification. Mac handed his SS card over, along with the forged letter from Himmler. The reichsführer's signature was enough to make the guard tremble. With a shaking hand, he returned the papers to Mac, jumped backward and, throwing his arm out straight, shouted, "Heil Hitler," and let them on through.

By the time they reached the city's outskirts, the sun had risen above the horizon. In its light, Nuremberg was a wretched sight. What had been the center of the Holy Roman Empire and one of the most beautiful cities in Europe lay in ruins. Harry's heart sank.

"You okay, Harry?" Mac whispered.

Harry didn't answer. He stared open mouth at the wreckage and the few civilians who picked through the rubble looking for some small piece of what had once been their lives. A tear slipped from his eye and rolled down his face.

"Harry?" Mac whispered. "SS officers don't cry."

Herschel touched his face where the tear streamed down and glanced at his damp fingers. Then he rubbed away any trace of the tear.

They came to a road blocked by a collapsed building. Roy stopped the Kübelwagen and turned around. "Herr Obersturmführer," he said, speaking bad German. "Which way? Herr Obersturmführer?"

Harry pulled himself from his fugue, looked around again, and frowned. "I—I'm not sure," he said, also in German. "Nothing looks the same. The landmarks …"

Mac pulled Peters' map of the city from under his tunic and studied it. "Go north as much as you can, Scharführer," he told Roy, also in German. "Eventually, we'll reach the old city and the castle."

The deeper into the city they drove, the worse the devastation. Center city—the medieval section where some of history's most significant persons once walked—lay in ashes. The twin steeples of the 13th century St. Sebaldus Church, where the famed organist Pachelbel played, were now skeletal specters, and the much older Church of St. Lorenz was all but demolished. Centuries of art and culture reduced to gray dust and the putrid miasma of death.

"Boy, they really clobbered this place," Roy muttered in English.

"You heard Peters," Harry said, looking around to make sure no one could hear them. "They wanted to destroy the heart of the Nazi Party."

"This may backfire on Seventh Army," Mac whispered. "All this rubble is going make it hell for Patch's troops to root out the kr—" Mac stopped himself. "Jerries."

"I just had a thought," Harry said. "What if the bunker is buried under a collapsed building?"

"It might be," Mac said. "In which case, we turn around and go back to the safehouse and call for Flaherty."

Eventually, they spotted the castle keeps still standing watch over the remains of the surrounding old city. Despite the rubble-strewn streets and battered facades of collapsed buildings, Harry began to get his bearings. Studying the map given him by the German POW Steinbrink, he was able to guide Damper to Blacksmith's Alley.

"That's it!" Harry said aloud in English. He checked himself and glanced around to see if anyone had heard. They were alone. "That's it," he said more calmly in German. "Number 52, the parking garage."

"Are you sure?" asked Roy. "I thought we were looking for an alley with a blacksmith."

"That was a long time ago," Harry said. "Now it's a street."

The building housing Corporal Steinbrink's family bakery was miraculously untouched by the bombing. Standing four stories tall, including the parking garage hiding the entrance to the bunker, it was squeezed on both sides by similar brick buildings with peaked roofs. A large arched entrance on the left allowed vehicles into the garage, while a smaller entrance to the right allowed pedestrians access to the upper floors.

Despite little damage to this section of the city, Blacksmith's Alley was vacant and eerily quiet. The three Americans glanced up and down the narrow street but saw no one.

"Shouldn't there be guards? Roy asked.

"They'd be in the garage, or maybe in the bunker itself," Harry said.

"Well, let's take a look," Mac said. "Scharführer, the door."

Roy jumped from the vehicle, slung his MP-40 over his shoulder, and rushed around to the right rear door and opened it. Harry stepped out, followed by Mac. Each straightened and dusted their tunics.

"Stay here, Scharführer," Mac said.

Roy clicked his heels. "Jawohl, Herr Obersturmbannführer!"

They strolled toward the garage, Harry walking to the left and slightly behind Mac, as an SS aide would do. The twin doors of the car park were locked. While Harry stood guard, Mac used a lock pick kit to open the doors. The garage was dark and empty. Standing in its center, they glanced one way, then the other, waiting for their eyes to adjust to the darkness.

"There," said Harry, pointing to the far-left corner where two large steel doors stood out from the brickwork.

They strode to the metal doors and examined them. There was no window, no buzzer to ring, no gun ports. Harry looked at Mac and asked, "How do we get in?"

Mac shrugged. "Try knocking."

Harry pulled his Walther from its holster and used the butt to pound on the door. They waited. Herschel pounded again. And still they waited. Harry again banged on the doors with his pistol, so hard he feared he might damage his only weapon. Again, they waited.

Harry holstered the Walther and shook his head.

"There must be someone in the city who knows how to get inside," he said.

There was a metallic thunk from inside the bunker. One of the doors groaned and creaked open. A guard in an SS uniform peered out from the crack.

"Ja, was ist es?" the guard asked warily. *Yes, what is it?*

Mac moved so the guard could see his uniform and rank emblems and held his SS ID card up to the soldier's face. "SS Obersturmbannführer Mendler and aide."

The guard's face blanched. He opened the door further, but not enough for Mac and Harry to enter. "Please wait here while I inform the sergeant of the guard, Herr Obersturmbannführer," he said, then closed the door.

Mac removed a glove and slapped it against his other hand while they waited. The door finally creaked open again, and the sergeant of the guard peered out. Mac held up his identification card and thrust the forged Himmler letter at the guard. "Read."

The sergeant removed the letter from its envelope and read it. He stiffened and clicked his heels, handed the letter and its envelope back, then pushed open the heavy door. "My apologies, Herr Obersturmbannführer," he said, "but we are under orders not to let anyone in. My corporal was only following orders."

"Of course," Mac said.

The sergeant squinted suspiciously at the garage doors. "Forgive me for asking, Obersturmbannführer, but how did you get into the garage? The doors were locked."

Mac and Harry glanced at each other. Mac slapped his hand with his glove again and gave the guard a malevolent smile.

"No, sergeant," he said. "They were not. And I was wondering about that security lapse myself."

"Verdammt!" the guard cursed. "I'll have Snyder's balls for that breach."

"As well you should, sergeant," Mac said. He waved the Himmler letter. "But to the matter at hand. I assume this provides my aide and me access?"

"But of course, Herr Obersturmbannführer!" The sergeant stood back from the door, clicked his heels again, and said, "Willkommen im Kunstbunker!" *Welcome to the art bunker!*

Chapter 11

THERE WAS A LOADING dock just inside the doors, then a long ramp leading deeper underground. The walls and ceiling of the tunnel were rough-hewn stone and expanded into a high, arched ceiling.

"An unusual bunker," Mac said.

"It was originally a beer cellar," the SS sergeant said. "It extends under the castle to where the royal brewery was. But as we continue, you will see many improvements were made."

They passed a guard station, barracks, and a latrine with showers. The tunnel grew more expansive, with rooms to the left and right, each sealed with a metal door. "These," the sergeant said, "were where the barrels of beer were stored. Now they store paintings and other artwork."

"I would think a beer cellar would not be ideal for storing art," Harry said.

"The obersturmführer is correct," the sergeant said. "The storage rooms would be too damp. But each chamber now has a false interior of insulated walls and ceiling, and as you can tell, the ventilation apparatus keeps us cool but dry."

"It is quite comfortable down here," Mac observed. "But sergeant, while I appreciate the pride you put into your responsibility here, we are pressed for time. As you read in Reichsführer Himmler's letter, we are here to ensure the Imperial Regalia are secure and safe."

"Jawohl, Herr Obersturmbannführer!" the guard said. "This way, please."

The sergeant led them down a long corridor that ended in a large metal door with two combination locks and a locking wheel the size of an automobile steering wheel. He stood to one side and extended his arm as if presenting a great find.

"Quite impressive," Mac said.

The guard's chest puffed out with pride.

Mac and Harry glanced at each other. Mac looked at the guard, and the guard looked back.

"So, may we?"

"Mein Herr?"

Mac waved his glove at the door. "May we enter?" he said. "We must examine the Imperial Regalia."

The guard deflated. "No, mein Herr."

"I beg your pardon?" Mac said, casting a stony stare at the sergeant.

"Forgive me, Herr Obersturmbannführer," the guard said, "but I do not have the combination to the vault."

Mac's stare turned icy. "Then who does?"

"I—I do not know, Herr Obersturmbannführer," the sergeant said.

"Then how do you check the contents?" Mac asked, his voice tightening.

The sergeant's mouth opened and shut several times like a landed fish gasping for air.

"I don't, Herr Obersturmbannführer," he said. "I have never been inside the vault. None of us have."

"Who, then, does enter the vault to check on the contents?"

"Herr Obersturmbannführer, I have seen no one go inside the Regalia vault. None of us have."

"Who is your commanding officer?" Mac asked.

"Untersturmführer Heinz was my commanding officer, Herr Obersturmbannführer."

"*Was*?"

"He was killed last week in a bombing raid," the sergeant said. "A bomb landed on our above-ground barracks. Several of our people were killed."

"Well, who is in command of the guard detail now?" Mac asked.

"I am, Herr Obersturmbannführer."

Mac took a long, deep breath, puffed his cheeks out, and blew it out.

"Let's start over, sergeant," he said. "We are here at the order of Reichsführer Himmler to verify the safety of the

Imperial Regalia. In order to do that, we need to get *inside* the Regalia vault and actually *see* the relics. You understand that, correct?"

"Jawohl, Herr Obersturmbannführer."

"Fine. That means we need to find who has the combination to the vault," Mac continued. "And you understand that?"

"Jawohl, Herr Obersturmbannführer!"

"Now, who would know who has the combination?"

The SS guard screwed up his face in thought, then said, "Perhaps Herr Kauffman, the curator of the art museum."

"Wilhem Kauffman?" asked Harry.

The sergeant nodded. "Herr Kauffman comes to inspect the artwork in the other storage vaults every week, sometimes more. He never goes into the Regalia vault, but he may know who has the combination."

Mac smiled but did little to calm the guard's nervousness. "Excellent, sergeant," he said. "Now, where might we find this Herr Kauffman?"

"At the art museum, I would assume, Herr Obersturmbannführer," the sergeant said.

"And the museum is where?" asked Mac.

"I know the way, Herr Obersturmbannführer," Harry said. "I visited there many times before the war."

Mac nodded. "Fine. Shall we go then?"

The sergeant escorted Mac and Harry to the bunker door.

"We shall see you again, sergeant," Mac said. He glanced at Harry and added *sotto voce*, "At least, I hope so."

The sergeant clicked his heels and saluted. "Heil Hitler!"

Mac returned the salute with a wave of his hand and left.

☼

"You know this Herr Kauffman?" Mac asked as they settled back in the Kübelwagen.

"I know *of* him," Harry said. "He taught art history at the university when I studied there. My father knew him pretty well, but mostly through correspondence. I've seen Kauffman around, but I don't think we were ever formally introduced."

"So, he won't recognize you?"

Harry thought about that awhile before shaking his head. "I doubt it. I was one of hundreds of students at the university. It's possible we ran across each other at a showing at the museum, but if we did, it wasn't anything memorable."

"How do we get to the museum?"

"Let me see Peters' map."

Mac took the map from his tunic and handed it to Herschel. He studied it for a minute, then gave Roy the directions. As they rode through the debris-strewn streets, Harry briefed Mac on what he remembered of Wilhem Kauffman. Though he never met the man, he remembered various comments his father said about him after reading some of his correspondence. The adjective his father most often used was "pompous," usually followed by one part of the lower human anatomy or another. He also remembered hearing similar remarks from some of Kauffman's students following his lectures. *Blodes Arschloch*—or "stupid asshole"—was the most frequently used term.

"Mac," he finally said. "May I make a suggestion?"

"Sure. What?"

"When we meet with Kauffman, let me do most of the talking," Harry said.

Mac eyed Herschel. "Why?"

"Kauffman's an art historian," Harry said. "The best way to get an art historian to cooperate with you is to pamper his ego." He turned to Mac and smiled. "Remember, my father was an art historian."

Mac grinned and laughed. "Sure, Harry, we'll do it your way," he said. "Fender did say you were a damn good interrogator."

Chapter 12

THE ART MUSEUM WAS only minutes away as the crow flies, but with the Kübelwagen, it took much longer. Many streets were cleared of rubble from the bombings, while others were only partially cleared, and others not cleared at all. Roy nosed the vehicle down some streets only to find their passage blocked by debris or barriers warning of unexploded bombs. With Harry's help, he finally pulled up to the art museum which stood on a street that, like Blacksmith's Alley, was miraculously untouched by the air attacks.

Roy leapt from the Kübelwagen and opened the door for Harry and Mac, then opened the door to the museum, which was unlocked. Mac strode in first, followed by Harry, while Roy remained with the vehicle as before.

The museum was void of both people and artwork. The walls were barren, light dust marks outlining where paintings once hung. Display cases stood empty and dusty. The only evidence of habitation was a muffled news report from an unseen radio.

Harry looked at Mac, who nodded. Harry raised his voice and said, "Hallo? Ist hier jemand?" *Hello? Is anyone here?*

The radio went quiet, then a voice replied in German, "I am sorry, but we are closed."

"Professor Kauffman?"

Footsteps echoed off the empty walls, an unnatural staccato step. A man appeared from a room, tall and thin, his clipped hair and moustache much grayer than Harry remembered. He walked with a pronounced limp and supported himself with a cane.

"Yes," the man said. "I am Professor Kauffman—" He stopped abruptly on seeing Harry and Mac, and snapped to attention, raising his right arm in a rigid salute. "Heil Hitler!"

Mac flipped his hand in a casual salute and replied, "Heil Hitler. Please, professor, stand at ease."

Kauffman relaxed. He smiled, revealing tobacco-stained teeth. "Gentlemen, to what do I owe this honor?"

"Professor, allow me to introduce Obersturmbannführer Mendler," Harry said. "And I am Obersturmführer Köhler, his aide."

Mac and Harry dipped their heads in a polite bow, which Kauffman returned. The curator examined Harry through his round, metal-framed glasses. "Have we met, Obersturmführer? You seem to know me."

"Only by reputation, professor," Harry said. "I studied at the university here before the war and sat in on many of your lectures."

Kauffman brightened. "You were an art student?"

"I was a student of history, professor," Harry said. "But also, a great admirer of art. And I must say, I found your lectures on the hedonism of the modern artists … quite stimulating."

Kauffman beamed. He removed his glasses and polished them with a handkerchief. "Yes, yes," he said. "The Führer was quite right to ban all that rubbish by degenerates like Paul Klee and Max Beckmann. Perfect examples of the influence Jews and Bolsheviks had on what might otherwise had been talented artists. Herr Hitler knows art, you know. He is an artist himself. I have had the great honor of viewing some of the early works he did before he took up politics. The world lost a talent of great potential when he did. Why, I remember …"

Mac cleared his throat and Kauffman fell silent.

"Professor," Harry said, "as much as I would enjoy spending the entire afternoon discussing art with you, I must tell you we are here on urgent business for the reichsführer."

Mac produced the forged Himmler letter and handed it to Harry, who presented it to Kauffman. The professor's eyes grew wide as he read the signature at the bottom of the letter.

"Of course. Of course," Kauffman said, handing the letter back to Harry. "I'm happy to help you in any way I can. Please, follow me to where we can sit."

Kauffman led them down a hallway into his office, which had a desk in one corner fronted by cushioned chairs and a small sofa. The room was neat but dusty, evidence of being rarely used in recent times. He directed them to the chairs.

"May I offer you some refreshment?" he asked. "I'm afraid I have no coffee—no one does these days—and the ersatz substitute is not worth drinking. I do have a bottle of schnapps ..."

Harry waved off the offer. "Perhaps another time, Herr Professor. I'm afraid this is an important matter, and we have so little time."

"Of course," Kaufmann said. As he limped toward his desk, he said, "You know, I am SS, too. Or was. I led one of the art retrieval teams in France until ..." He tapped his bad leg with his cane. "Partisans." He spit the word out.

"Treacherous bastards," Mac said.

"Quite correct." Kauffman lowered himself with care into his desk chair, hooked the cane on the chair back, then folded his hands in front of him on the desk. "Now, then, gentlemen, how may I help you?"

"As the reichsführer's letter says, we are here to verify the security of the Imperial Regalia," Harry said. "Unfortunately, we are unable to complete our assignment."

Kauffmann's hands unfolded like butterfly wings. "But why not?" he asked. "Surely, it is all secured in the vault. It is merely a matter of looking inside."

"Exactly," Harry said. "But that is the problem. We are unable to open the vault. The sergeant of the guard does not have the combination and his officer is dead—killed by the bombings. He suggested you might know how to get inside?"

"Me?"

"He said you visit regularly."

The curator nodded. "Yes, yes," he said. "But that is only to check on the museum's artwork stored in the other vaults. Those are my responsibility and I have keys for them. The Holy Relics, however, are not my responsibility."

Mac and Harry glanced at each other. Mac frowned. "Then, Herr Professor, whose responsibility are they?" he demanded.

"Why, the mayor's," Kauffmann said. "Willy Liebel. The regalia was in the city's legal possession. So, the responsibility lies with the mayor."

"Where can we find Mayor Liebel?" asked Harry.

Kauffman threw up his hands. "Ach! Who knows? No one has seen him for more than a week. He has not been to his office nor his home. He may be in hiding because of bombing. He may be dead, buried under the rubble. So many thousands have died from the bombs, you know. The

RAF are such pigs." Kauffman frowned and his voice became full of distain. "Or he may have left the city, run away from his responsibilities as a German and party member—like too many others, if I may be so direct. So many cowards! No sense of duty to the Führer, the dogs."

Mac and Harry looked at each other again. "That does leave us in a predicament," Harry said. "If we can't find the mayor, we can't open the vault and verify the safety and security of the regalia. We can't complete our duty. The reichsführer will not be happy."

Mac stood, clicked his heels, and bowed toward the curator. "Herr Professor, we've taken up enough of your time. We must be leaving. Thank you."

Harry stood and imitated Mac's bow. They turned and started for the door.

"Gentlemen?" Kauffman tapped his lips with a finger.

"Yes, Herr Professor?" Harry said.

Kauffmann pursed his lips in thought, then asked, "To complete your assignment, all you need is to *see* the relics. Am I correct?"

"Herr Professor?"

"You don't have to remove them, do you?"

"No, Herr Professor," Harry said. He glanced at Mac, whose eyes narrowed.

"Well," the curator said. "There is another way into the Regalia vault. Actually, more of a way *out* of the vault."

Chapter 13

MAC AND HARRY EYED each other, then as one asked, "Professor?"

"The emergency escape," Kauffmann said. "It was feared that the building above the secret entrance might collapse during a bombing and seal it, trapping the guards and the artwork. The bunker's design called for three escape tunnels to the surface so the guard detail could escape but also—" The curator pointed a finger toward the ceiling, then curved it toward the floor. "So, we could go *in* and retrieve the artwork, if needed."

"But do they provide access to the Imperial Regalia vault, professor?" Harry asked.

Kauffmann laid his hands out, palms up, as if the problem was solved. "One does." Two fingers on his right hand wiggled as he lowered them toward the floor. "So, all you need do is climb down the escape tunnel and check on the relics."

"You know where this escape tunnel is located and how to access it?" Mac asked.

"Not off the top of my head," the curator said. "But I have the blueprints for the bunker here in my office. I was consulted on the storage requirements for the artwork when it was built. Now where did I put them?"

Harry's fingers tapped an impatient beat on his trouser leg as Kauffmann hobbled around his office peeking into desk drawers, filing cabinets, and cubbyholes. Mac stayed stoic, but his eyes followed every movement the professor made.

"You must forgive me, gentlemen," Kauffmann said. "Normally, I would have my secretary retrieve any papers I needed. Unfortunately, she was lost in one of the raids. Ah! Here they are."

The curator drew from a file cabinet a roll of bluish documents, limped back to his desk, and spread them out. Mac and Harry stepped closer as he flipped through the pages, stopping twice to place a finger to show the location of an escape tunnel.

"Yes, yes," he finally said, throwing aside the other pages, jabbing the remaining page with a finger and waving the other two men closer. "Here, the escape tunnel leading out of—and *into*—the relics vault."

Both men leaned in as Kauffman's finger traced the outline of the escape tunnel. "Where, Herr Professor, does it come out?" asked Mac.

"Hmmmm," Kauffman murmured as he deciphered the blueprints. "Ah, yes, yes, I remember now. There was already a concealed entrance to the beer cellar the clergy used in their work. It was decided to build the Imperial vault around it and use the clerics' entrance as an escape tunnel."

"But where does it come out, Herr Professor?" Mac repeated.

"It comes out in the Knight's Hall."

"And that would be where?" Mac asked.

"Nuremberg Castle, Herr Obersturmbannführer," Harry answered.

"Exactly. It is where the Holy Roman emperors were greeted on their arrival when holding court in Nuremberg," Kauffmann said. Then he knitted his brow, remembering. "Oh, that section of the castle was recently damaged in the bombing."

"Meaning?" Mac demanded.

"It may be difficult to find the escape hatch," the curator said. "It may be hidden by debris."

Mac turned to Harry. "You know how to find this Knights Hall?" Harry nodded. "Then we will find it." He turned to Kauffman. "Herr Professor, I thank you for your time and this information."

Mac and Harry turned to leave, but Kauffmann stopped them.

"Gentlemen, I am very knowledgeable about the castle," he said. "I would be happy to join you in your search."

Harry looked at Mac who gave him a quick, almost imperceptible frown. "Thank you, Herr Professor," Harry said, "but the reichsführer awaits our report, and I am afraid your wound would only slow us down. You know how impatient the reichsführer can be."

Kauffmann looked crestfallen, but he straightened himself and nodded curtly. "Of course, of course. Herr Himmler must not be kept waiting. Good day, gentlemen, and good hunting. Heil Hitler."

Mac and Harry returned the salute and left.

Built on a sandstone ridge, the imperial castle's three towers watched over the city like ancient sentinels, while the massive protective stone walls surrounding it hunched below. Yet even from street level, it was obvious the towers and the walls could not protect the castle from falling British bombs. Portions of the roof of the Palas, which housed the Knight's Hall, were missing.

After several detours, they reached the street leading to the castle. Troops on foot and horse-drawn artillery limbers and their caissons clogged the road. A feldgendarmerie, or military policeman, directing traffic at the intersection stopped them. Spotting their SS uniforms, he stiffened and raised his arm in salute.

"I am sorry, Herr Obersturmbannführer," the policeman said. "But the castle is being fortified and accessible only to military traffic.

Mac returned a casual salute. "As I understand," he said. "However, we are here on direct orders from the reichsführer. Let us pass."

"But Herr Obersturmbannführer," the soldier begged, "my orders."

Mac's eyes rolled with impatience. He reached into his tunic, withdrew the forged letter, and handed it to the MP. "My orders."

The MP's eyes widened at the signature, and he handed it back quietly as if it were poisonous. "Yes, of course, Herr Obersturmbannführer," he said, saluting again. "Proceed."

The feldgendarmerie stepped into the flow of traffic, blowing a whistle and raising his hand to stop the oncoming traffic, then waved the Kübelwagen to join the convoy.

Roy followed the convoy up the long, narrow street toward the castle and into its stonework walls. The narrow path between the walls and the towers, twin chapels, and Palas was claustrophobic and littered with debris. Harry tapped him on the shoulder and pointed to a spot below the Palas.

"Park there," he whispered.

Roy pulled out of the convoy and parked. He pulled a tool bag out as they left the vehicle and walked into the heart of the castle, past the Heidenturm, or Heathen's Tower, and the Imperial Chapel into the outer courtyard. There another feldgendarmerie stopped them.

"I apologize, Herr Obersturmbannführer," he said, "but it is dangerous here." He pointed to a sign propped against the door leading to Knights' Hall that read: Nicht Explodierte Bombe. *Unexploded Bomb.* "The bastard British. We are waiting for the bomb technician."

"He is here," Mac said, waving toward Roy and his tool bag. "He is our explosives expert."

Roy and Harry looked askance at each other but said nothing.

A look of relief appeared on the policeman's face. "Of course, Herr Obersturmbannführer, please proceed."

As the team entered the hall, the feldgendarmerie took several quick steps backward to what he hoped was a safe distance.

"Mac, are you crazy?" Roy muttered. "I'm no bomb technician."

"I didn't say you were," Mac replied. "I said you were my explosives expert. And you are."

"I blow things up," Roy protested. "I don't disarm bombs."

"And you're not going to," Mac said. "We just find the escape tunnel, grab the spear, and leave. By the time the real bomb technician shows up, we'll be gone."

"And what if the bomb goes off while we're looking for the hatch?" Roy asked.

Mac shrugged. "Either way, we'll be gone before the bomb technician gets here."

Harry entered the hall first and froze, horrified by the sight. At its height, a ceiling held aloft by thirty massive beams set crosswise on a colossal joist supported by five carved oak columns dominated the Knights' Hall. To one side, an entire wall of windows overlooked Nuremberg. At its east end, stairs led through an arched doorway into the Imperial Chapel, one of two churches in the castle. Above the archway was a depiction of Christ as Judge. On either side were renderings of Emperor Friedrich III with the Hapsburg coat of arms, and Maximilian I bearing the Habsburg-Burgundy coat of arms. Now, all of that was in ruin.

Much of the grand ceiling now littered the floor. The windows overlooking the city were blown out; only shards of glass grimed with dust from the blasted stonework remained. Dust also obscured the renderings of Christ and the emperors. Brickwork joined the remains of the ceiling on the floor, and in the middle of it all was an enormous crater from which protruded the fins of a five-hundred-pound British bomb.

"Harry, what's wrong?" Mac whispered.

Harry tore himself from his fugue and shook his head. "Nothing. Nothing," he said. "Just … nothing."

"Jesus," Roy said, "Where do we start looking?"

Harry pulled the hand-drawn map Corporal Steinbrink gave him and studied it. He held the map up, turning it one way, then the next. Finally, he folded the map and put it away. "The other side of the bomb," he said, pointing. "That's where the bunker extends under the castle."

"You sure?" Mac asked.

"It makes sense," Harry said. "The clerics were tasked with brewing and maintaining the royal beer supply, and that door at the far end leads to a chapel. It would've been a shortcut into the beer cellar for them."

They inched their way through the debris toward the windows and stepped around the bomb crater. Roy crossed himself as he crept past the bomb.

"Hey, Roy, you think this thing could be a dud?" Harry asked.

"Like I said, I'm no bomb technician," Roy said. "But I was having drinks one night with a British UXO guy who—"

"UXO?" Harry questioned.

"Unexploded ordnance," Mac said.

"He defused German bombs dropped on London," Roy continued. "He said in a situation like this, the bomb was either a dud or it had a delayed fuse."

"Meaning?"

"Meaning it could explode hours, days, even weeks after landing," Mac answered.

"But if it's a dud, it won't explode, right?" Just as Harry asked, a plank gave way under his weight with a thunderous crack. Mac grabbed him before Harry tumbled into the crater.

"Only if you don't disturb it," Roy said, shaking his head.

Reaching the east end of the hall, they began sifting through debris, stomping the floor for the dull thump of a hollow. At times, it took all three of them to heave broken ceiling beams out of the way. Each step or movement raised a cloud of brick dust that coated their uniforms. After nearly a half hour of searching, they were ready to give up.

Harry removed his peaked cap and wiped his brow with his sleeve. It left a gray smear of dust on his forehead. "Maybe we should have let the old man come with us."

Mac simply shook his head.

Roy unslung his Schmeisser and leaned it against the wall. He then snatched the Stahlhelm off his head and tossed it next to the submachine gun. The steel helmet struck the wall with a hollow thud, then landed on the debris-strewn floor, wobbled on its crown, then settled.

Mac and Harry both slowly turned and looked at the helmet. Mac bent down, picked up the Stahlhelm, and started banging it up and down the wall. Most of the wall returned a solid clunk. But the spot where Roy's Strahlhelm had struck returned another hollow thud. Mac banged the helmet against the wall again, and soon had the outline of what looked like a doorway.

"This is it," Mac said. He pressed against the wall, but nothing moved.

"You want me to blow it open, Mac?" Roy asked.

"With that thing fifteen feet away?" Harry protested, pointing to the bomb.

"Any better suggestions?" Mac asked.

Harry looked around, frowning. Then he shook his head. "Like I said, the clerics were responsible for maintaining the beer cellar. They would have camouflaged the entrance so servants and staff couldn't get in and help themselves to a drink. But they wouldn't have made it difficult for themselves to get in. So, there must be a locking lever concealed nearby. Look for anything that could be a disguised lever."

It didn't take long to find it. Scanning the wall, Harry spied a replica of the Holy Roman cross hanging on the wall. All other wall hangings in the hall had been thrown or displaced from their perches by the bombing, yet this particular cross, covered with dust, remained undisturbed. He grabbed the cross and pulled, but it didn't move. Then he tried to turn it and it gave way with a clunk. Harry turned to Mac and nodded.

Mac leaned into the portion of hollow wall he'd outlined. One side moved inward. He continued pushing, and it swung open.

"Well, I'll be damned," Roy muttered.

Chapter 14

THE DOOR OPENED ONTO a narrow vestibule. On the floor was an airtight hatch with a dogging wheel.

Mac looked at Harry. "An airtight seal in case of gas attack?" Harry guessed.

"You mean the monks didn't install this?" Mac said with a smirk.

"It probably had a bit of updating," Harry conceded.

Mac squatted over the hatch, turned the wheel, and lifted it. Stale air greeted their nostrils. Roy handed him a flashlight from the tool bag and Mac shone it down the shaft. Harry was right; past the airtight hatch, the shaft had been roughly hand hewn through the castle's foundation. Ancient iron bolts seated in the side of the shaft still held bits of a wooden ladder, now replaced by a steel ladder secured by newer bolts.

"Roy, stay up here and close that door behind us," Mac said, then lowered himself into the shaft.

Harry followed Mac into the darkness, and Roy closed the concealed door. Harry climbed down the ladder by feel, the only light being the flashlight Mac held. The air smelled of unfinished wood, dried grass, and old clothing. Finally, his foot touched the vault floor, and he looked around.

The beam of Mac's torch revealed a room perhaps thirty feet long and half as wide, crammed with wooden crates. As the flashlight flitted across the boxes, Harry saw each crate was numbered and had a packing label attached identifying its contents. Taking the light from Mac, Harry walked along the single, narrow aisle that gave access to the boxes, reading each label. Crate ten had been opened and emptied, its lid carelessly tossed aside. Packing straw littered the ground. Further on, a crate numbered fifteen also stood open and empty. Next to crate ten was a space where crate eleven once sat, now missing.

"This doesn't make sense," he said. "According to these packing labels, some of the most precious of the imperial relics were removed. The imperial crown, the scepter and orb, and both imperial swords. Who would do that and why?"

"What about the spear?" Mac asked.

Harry hesitated a moment, still shocked by the theft of the relics, then said, "Over here."

He stepped over to one of the smaller crates, took the SS dagger hanging from his belt, and pried off the lid. Carefully scooping the straw aside, he found a smaller wooden box. He removed the box, placed it on another crate, and opened it.

The Spear of Destiny shone dully in the flashlight's beam. Harry stared at it, shaking his head. "Why take the others and leave this? It doesn't make sense."

"It doesn't matter," Mac said, impatient. "What matters is we've got the spear. Let's go."

"Not yet," Harry said. "Give me a moment. I need to verify its authenticity." He looked at Mac, who didn't move. "I need to do it *alone*."

Mac rolled his eyes and sighed in exasperation. "Fine," he said, moving off into the darkness.

Five minutes later, Harry walked up to Mac without the spear. "It's a fake," he said.

"A fake?" said Mac. "How can that be? What about the other relics?"

"Whoever took the crown and scepter and the other items had to know the spear wasn't real."

"But your father said the spear in Vienna—"

"I know what he said," Harry said. "But that's not the one he authenticated."

"Could the real spear be in another crate?" Mac asked.

Harry shook his head, though Mac couldn't see it in the dark. "I searched the crate it was in. The fake spear was the only thing in it. All the other crates have detailed packing inventories. Someone must have switched the real spear for the fake sometime after the Nazis confiscated the regalia. What do we do now, Mac?"

Mac took the flashlight and headed toward the escape ladder. "We get the hell out of here right now, that's what we do," he said.

It was nearing sunset when they wended their way through the chaotic city streets to the same southern road they used to enter Nuremberg. Military traffic still crowded the northbound lanes, but the lanes leading from the city were relatively barren. An occasional abandoned civilian vehicle littered the roadside. Now and then, they passed civilian refugees laden with whatever pieces of their lives they could salvage from their bombed and battered houses. Most were leaving the city but, curiously, a growing number were heading back to Nuremberg.

"You'd think with an attack coming, more civilians would try to leave the city," Harry said.

Mac grunted, his eyes scanning the roadside.

They came to another derelict automobile. Inside were two bodies in civilian clothes, both obviously shot in the head at close range. All three stared at the victims as they passed. Harry heard a soft snap and saw Mac release the flap of his pistol holster. At the same time, Roy reached for his Schmeisser and pulled it closer to him. Mac glanced at Harry and dipped his head, indicating Harry's holster. Harry swallowed hard and unsnapped the holster's flap.

A minute later, they saw the problem.

A roadblock was stopping all outgoing traffic. Even from a distance, they could see small clumps of civilians forced to turn around and trudge back toward the city. Those with vehicles were forced to abandon them and walk back to Nuremberg.

"What do we do, Mac?" Roy asked. "Want me to cut across country?"

"No, we do that now, and they'll just chase after us," Mac said. "Best bet is to play it straight and hope Himmler's signature scares them like the others."

Roy nosed the Kübelwagen up to the barricade, which consisted of a long two-by-four propped up on two saw-horses. A squad of heavily armed Feldgendarmerie manned the barricade, led by a stern *oberleutnant*, or first lieutenant. The officer approached the Kübelwagen and gave a half-hearted salute that Harry took as an omen.

"Nobody leaves the city," the lieutenant said. "You must turn about, Herr Obersturmbannführer."

"We are under direct orders from Reichsführer Himmler," Mac said, producing the forged letter. "We must report back to him immediately."

The field policeman glanced at the letter, then handed it back.

"Nobody leaves the city," he repeated.

"By whose orders?" Mac demanded.

"Herr Karl Holz, Reich defense commissioner and gauleiter of this region," the lieutenant said. "Everybody stays and fights. Helmets and weapons are being issued to all citizens of Nuremberg."

"You place a gauleiter, a civilian appointee, above the reichsführer?" Mac said.

"I do not take my orders from the reichsführer," the officer said. "The Führer himself placed Herr Holz in charge of the city's defense, and Herr Holz answers only to him. And I answer only to Herr Holz. Now, you will exit the vehicle."

"Exit the vehicle?" Mac said. His right hand, concealed by his left arm, tightened on the butt of his Walther. "Why?"

"We have need of it," the lieutenant said. "You can commandeer any of those vehicles …" He pointed to the military trucks rolling toward the city. "To return you to the city."

Mac shook his head. His eyes were slits of doubt. "How do I know you won't use it to flee the city yourself?" Mac said. He nodded to the other Feldgen. "You and your men?"

Accusing him of cowardice and treason outraged the oberleutnant. His face reddened, and he glared at Mac as he moved to unsnap his pistol holster. "Exit the vehicle now!" he demanded.

Mac's right arm swung up. The German officer barely had time to register the Walther in his hand before Mac shot him twice in the head. At the same instant, Roy raised the Schmeisser with one hand and fired a burst at the other Feldgendarmerie as the Kübelwagen leapt forward. The field policemen jumped out of the way as the vehicle crashed through their barricade. Harry fired his Walther as they passed the stunned policemen. Roy backhanded the Schmeisser to Mac, who, facing backward, sprayed the remaining Feldgendarmerie left in their wake. The Kübelwagen roared down the road and disappeared into the dimming light.

Chapter 15

"PATTON'S NOT HAPPY, BOYS," Fender said as he returned to the OSS barracks.

"Yeah, we thought we heard him all the way over here," Roy quipped.

They had been back one day from their mission to Nuremberg. After evading the Feldgendarmerie roadblock, they turned off the road and drove cross-country, eventually dumping the Kübelwagen in the forest and making their way back to the safe house on foot. The following night, Flaherty landed his Lysander in a different field than the one they arrived in, taxied to the end of the clearing, and pivoted.

"Come along, lads," he called out, banging the outside of his cockpit with his hands.

Mac, Roy, and Harry scrambled up the boarding ladder. This time, Harry declined Mac's invitation to sit in the rear cockpit, preferring to remain oblivious to the anti-aircraft fire the Germans hurled at them on the return trip. Now they sat in the barracks in their regular uniforms, sipping from another of Fender's bottles of scotch, and waiting to hear what George Patton's reaction would be upon hearing the Spear of Destiny he sent them after was fake.

"You very well may have heard Patton," Fender said, grabbing the scotch and pouring himself a long measure. He swallowed that in one gulp and poured another. "He did not take it well at all. I may need to go to medical and have my hearing checked. Perhaps when this war is over, I can file a disability claim."

"It's just an old lance blade," Roy muttered. "What's his problem?"

"It's a relic, an artifact," Mac said, remembering the OSS profile on Patton he had read. "He's been picking up artifacts and shipping them home since North Africa."

Harry, who had been lying on a bunk deep in thought, sat up. "He can't do that. It's illegal."

"Rank has its privileges," Mac said, taking the bottle from Fender and pouring himself another drink.

"It's more than that," Fender said. "Patton actually believes in the spear's legend. He said he once wrote a poem about the spear."

"Crazy old man," Roy said.

"That crazy old man believes we need the spear to win the war," Fender added.

"We're already winning it, sir," Roy said. "Anyone tell Patton?"

"You know, I did point that out to him, sergeant," Fender said. "He said as long as Hitler has the spear, nothing was certain." Fender raised his finger like a schoolteacher making a point. "And then he added we needed the spear to beat the Reds."

"Doesn't he know they're our allies?" Roy said.

"For now," Fender said. "The general said if we don't find the spear, the—and I quote—'the commie bastards will, and they'll use it to spread their atheistic commie horse shit around the world, including America.'"

"Well, what the hell can we do?" Mac said. "We don't know where it is. It could be anywhere in Germany."

"Or South America," Fender said. "Counter-intelligence says the Nazi leadership is setting up escape routes to friendly countries like Spain and Argentina."

Mac sat roughly in a wooden chair, splashing his drink. He threw up his free hand in exasperation. "Well, there you have it. Case closed."

"Maybe not," Harry murmured, again looking like his mind was elsewhere.

"What was that, lieutenant?" Fender asked.

Harry snapped from his reverie. "I said maybe not, sir," he said. "I'd bet the spear is still in Germany."

"Why?" Fender said. "Explain."

"When the Nazis confiscated the Imperial Regalia and took it to Nuremberg, they put it on display for everyone to see. But Hitler wasn't interested in the regalia itself, just one piece of it—the Holy Spear." Harry took his small notebook from his pocket and flipped through it. "Remember that quote from Hitler when he saw the spear for the first time?" He read from the notebook. "'I felt as though I myself had held it in my hands before in some earlier century of history—that I myself had once claimed it as my talisman of power and held the destiny of the world in my hands.'" He closed the notepad and placed it back in his pocket.

"So?"

"I'm guessing Hitler stole the spear and replaced it with the fake," Harry said. "That's why the fake spear was left behind. Hitler must have given the order to move only some of the regalia—the most important pieces—to another, safer location. But he didn't order the spear to be moved because he knew it was a fake."

"Where would Hitler get a fake spear?" Fender asked.

"He had one, sir," Mac said. "Remember, Harry said Himmler gave Hitler a replica of the spear before the war— before the Anschluss—with a promise that someday he would own the genuine article."

Harry looked at Mac. "My god, you *were* listening," Harry said with mock shock.

"I must've woken up from my nap at some point," Mac said.

"So, you believe Hitler has the spear with him in Berlin?" Fender asked. "In the Führer Bunker? Then it'll be in Russian hands soon."

"No, sir, I don't," Harry said. "I think he would store it—probably hide it—somewhere more personal. Somewhere where he'd have access to it alone. Not the bunker or his offices in Berlin, or even his personal apartment in Berlin. All of those are technically the property of the government or the Nazi Party. He'd want to keep it someplace he considered his own."

"Which would be …?" Fender asked.

"The Berghof, in the Bavarian Alps near Berchtesgaden," Harry said. "Hitler purchased the original structure there in the mid-thirties with the royalties from his book, *Mein Kampf*, and had it torn down and replaced with a mountain villa."

Fender nodded. "I know about the Berghof."

"Hitler spent more time there than anywhere else," Harry continued. "It was his special getaway, and he was very possessive of it, often pointing out that *he* bought it with *his* own money. He was very touchy about it because before he became chancellor, the government investigated him for tax fraud because so much of everything he seemed to have was owned by the party."

"If you're thinking about parachuting into the middle of Hitler's private residence, forget it," said Mac. "The place must be swarming with SS bodyguards."

"Not anymore," Fender said, shaking his head. "Third Infantry and the French Second Armored captured

Berchtesgaden two days ago, along with the 101st Airborne. But the Berghof must be a wreck. About a week ago, the RAF bombed the whole area, and we have reports that what was left was torched by retreating SS."

Fender sipped his scotch as he paced the room. He turned to Harry. "But you're saying it might still be there?"

Harry shrugged. "If it's hidden well enough to avoid being looted …"

"And if the RAF didn't blow it all to hell," Mac said. "Let's not forget that."

"I would think the Berghof has an air-raid bunker," Harry said. "That'd be the safest place to hide it."

Mac and Roy both gave Harry a pained look. Fender's face brightened. He downed his drink and picked up his helmet. "Standby, boys," he said, opening the door. "I'm heading back into the lion's den."

When the door closed, Roy lay on a bunk and covered his face with a pillow. His voice muffled, he said, "Harry, if you want to get me killed, just push down on this pillow. Hard."

Mac sat with his elbow resting on the table and his hand covering his eyes. "Harry," he sighed, shaking his head. "Harry. Harry."

Herschel opened his mouth to speak, then closed it. He repeated that two more times before saying, "I was just hypothesizing. I wasn't suggesting we actually go looking for it."

"Just push real hard, Harry," Roy said, pointing to the pillow over his face. "I won't fight you."

Mac finished his drink and stood looking at Harry with the same pained expression, then shook his head and left the room.

"Come on, Harry," Roy said. "Just one good push …"

PART TWO

The Pure Fools

<h1 style="text-align:center">Chapter 16</h1>

FOR A FEW BRIEF minutes, there was quiet.

No cannon fired. No bomb fell. Nothing exploded. One might have heard birds singing, if there were any birds left in Berlin.

SS Sturmbannführer Hans Steiner stepped out of the ruined café that served as his command post and glanced around. His next in command, a SS *hauptsturmführer* or captain, stepped up beside him.

"Was ist lose, Herr Sturmbannführer?" *What's up, major?*

"I'm not sure, Franz," Steiner said. "Perhaps the war is over—or maybe we're already dead."

Franz Rockenhäuser snorted and lit a cigarette, one of the few he had left. "Don't toy with me, Hans," he said, *sotto voce*. "Either would be too good to wish for."

Steiner smiled and slapped Rockenhäuser on the shoulder. "Don't worry, Franz. It won't last."

As if he were overheard, the crunch of distant cannon fire shattered the silence, and within moments the streets of outer Berlin erupted in a volley of explosions. Steiner and Rockenhäuser leapt back into the café ruins and huddled together against a remaining wall.

"Gottverdammt!" Rockenhäuser said through clenched teeth. "Sometimes your insight is just too damn good, Hans."

The bombardment subsided, the walking barrage moving away. The two men rose to their feet and made a vain attempt to dust off their uniforms. A courier stumbled into the café, his muddied uniform stained with fresh blood.

"Sturmbannführer Steiner?" the courier mumbled as he gave a trembling salute.

"I am," Steiner said. Then, after spotting the amount of blood on the soldier's uniform, exclaimed, *"Mein Gott!* Are you seriously injured?"

"Nein," the courier said. "It's my comrade's blood, sir. The barrage—he ..." The soldier swallowed hard. "Nothing left of him. The reichsführer sent two of us to make sure this got through to you."

The soldier reached into his courier pouch and handed Steiner an envelope sealed with Himmler's personal stamp.

"The reichsführer?" Steiner looked at Rockenhäuser. The adjutant's widened eyes stood out against his grimed face. The senior SS officer tore open the envelope and read the message. "I'm to report to Himmler's headquarters immediately."

He handed the letter to Rockenhäuser, who read it and said, "What do you think? Good news or bad?"

"Good news never comes out of Himmler's office," Steiner said. "Soldier." The courier straightened and clicked his heels. "Did you come by foot?"

"No, sir," the soldier said. "I have a motorcycle and sidecar."

"Good," Steiner said. "You'll take me to the reichsführer."

"Ah, Steiner, you are here."

Steiner clicked his heels and offered the Nazi straight-arm salute. "Reporting as ordered, Herr Reichsführer."

"Good. Good. Please stand at ease."

Himmler rose from his chair and walked around his desk. He wore an immaculate black SS dress uniform, which contrasted with Steiner's filthy field-gray battle dress.

Himmler picked up a display box and handed it to the SS officer.

"Do you know what this is?"

Steiner studied the object inside the box, a dark-gray, broken blade wrapped in a sheath of gold.

"I believe it is called the Spear of Destiny, Herr Reichsführer," Steiner said. "I saw it once when it was displayed in Nuremberg before the war."

"Quite right. Quite right," Himmler said. "This is your next assignment, sturmbannführer. To retrieve the actual Spear of Destiny. This is merely a replica."

"If I may ask, Herr Reichsführer," Steiner said, "isn't it still in Nuremberg with the rest of the Imperial Regalia?"

Himmler took a deep breath, frowned, then sighed. "Unfortunately, no. Are you familiar with the legend of the spear?"

"Only what I read about it when it was on display," Steiner said.

Himmler frowned. "One would think a senior SS officer would at least be familiar with the Führer's favorite Wagner opera."

"My apologies, Reichsführer," Steiner said. "I am afraid I'm not musically inclined. Which opera is that?"

"*Parsifal*," Himmler said. "It is the telling of the Spear of Destiny legend." He took the display box from Steiner's hand and studied it. "It is said whoever holds the spear holds his own destiny in his hands," he said. "The destiny of a great conqueror. But if he loses the spear ..." He let the box drop onto his desk. "He loses all he once won."

"Yes, Herr Reichsführer," Steiner said. "That is what I read."

"Some time ago, the Führer and I decided the spear was far too valuable to be on public display," Himmler said. "We replaced it with a duplicate—one of three I had made, like this one." He tapped the display box. "The True Spear was placed in safe keeping for the Führer. Unfortunately, the place where we hid the spear was overrun by the Amis before we could save it. You, my dear Steiner, and a few of your little band of commandos, are going to retrieve it."

"May I ask where and how, Herr Reichsführer?" Steiner asked.

"You will be informed of the where and the how by Obersturmbannführer Skorzeny later," Himmler said. "Before that, I want to emphasize to you how important this mission is."

Himmler paced the room a moment, his hands clasped behind his back, his head tilted upward as if sniffing the air.

"Before I continue, Steiner," he said, "I want you to understand that whatever is said in this room does not leave this room. Is that understood?"

"Jawohl, Herr Reichsführer!" Steiner said, clicking his heels for emphasis.

"Good, because if anything I say does leave this room," Himmler turned and glared at Steiner, "you will be shot."

"Of course, Herr Reichsführer."

Himmler unclasped his hands. The thin mouth beneath the tiny moustache turned down. "What I am about to tell you gives me no pleasure. It is like ashes in my mouth. But it cannot be denied. Germany is losing the war."

What Himmler said was no surprise to Steiner; he had long figured that himself. But to hear those words from the reichsführer himself was like a kick in the stomach. He felt he should protest, to tell Himmler all was not lost, but he didn't believe that himself and he was certain Himmler didn't either. So, he remained quiet.

Himmler eyed Steiner. "I take it from your silence the news does not shock you," he said. Now Steiner did begin to protest, but the reichsführer raised a hand to silence him. "Unfortunately, it doesn't shock many people these days. However, there is one last thing we can do to save Germany and the party—make a separate truce with the western Allies, the Americans, the British, even the French." His face pinched in distaste at the mention of the French. He raised his hand in a fist and said, "Then together we turn to the east and wipe Stalin and his red hordes off the face of the map. Does that idea shock you?"

Steiner swallowed hard. "Yes, it does, Herr Reichsführer," he said.

"Good. It should," Himmler said. "But negotiations are already underway with the help of intermediaries in Switzerland. I—that is, the Führer and I—believe a truce will soon be achievable. But that will still leave the Great Bear to the East to deal with. You know as I do, Stalin has amassed a massive army against us. Even with the Amis and the Tommies on our side, it will be difficult to defeat it. The

Führer needs every weapon at his disposal, no matter how revolutionary or *legendary*. We have new wonder weapons coming, more amazing and powerful than the V-2, but sometimes it takes more than weapons and men to win a battle. Sometimes it takes faith."

Himmler stepped to his desk and picked up the replica of the Spear of Destiny. "The Führer has total belief in the power of the Holy Spear, and he wishes to have it with him." He raised the spear above his head. "To hold it in his hand as he leads Germany into the final battle against evil."

Steiner made a nervous sound as he cleared his throat. "If I may, Herr Reichsführer, the Russians are already on our doorstep, banging on the door. What if there is no time to make a separate peace?"

Himmler dropped the lance head, turned, and scowled at Steiner. At that moment, Steiner was certain his destiny included a firing squad. Then the reichsführer's countenance softened. He frowned but nodded. "A fair question, Steiner," he said. "An impertinent question, but a fair one."

He linked his hands behind his back and paced again. "Germany may lose the war, but the party will not surrender. It must survive." He considered his words, then continued. "There are already plans in place to ensure its survival. Key individuals—mostly from the SS—have been dispatched to other parts of the world to ensure National

Socialism lives on. Should we fail here, the need for the spear is required to continue our heroic quest."

The reichsführer stepped up to Steiner, close enough for him to smell the schnapps on Himmler's breath. "And we need it for ourselves, the SS, the prime of the Fatherland's manhood. It is part of our heritage and our legacy. And it is our future as well! Do you understand?"

"Yes, Herr Reichsführer," Steiner said, because there was nothing else he could say.

"Very well, then," Himmler said. "Obersturmbannführer Skorzeny is waiting for you in the planning room. He will brief you on your mission. You are dismissed."

Steiner clicked his heels and raised his arm in salute. "Heil Hitler!"

Himmler watched with distaste as Steiner marched from the office, his soiled battle dress leaving behind small dust clouds of dirt. As the door closed, he allowed himself a small smile of pleasure. Soon, assuming Steiner succeeded in his mission, he would once more hold the Holy Lance in his hands. Its power would be his again and he, not Hitler, would lead Germany to victory against the east. He, and not Hitler, was the man of destiny who would lead the Third Reich into a thousand years of greatness.

Chapter 17

STANDING SIX-FOOT-FOUR, broad shouldered and barrel-chested, Obersturmbannführer Otto Skorzeny was a large man with thick dark hair, rugged good looks, and a dueling scar that ran down his left cheek. Despite his not insignificant stature, Skorzeny's legend and the reputation behind it were even grander.

The Austrian-born Waffen-SS officer served heroically on the Eastern Front, earning the Iron Cross, second class, until he was put out of action when struck in the back of the head by shrapnel. While recovering from his wound, Skorzeny organized his thoughts on unconventional warfare. Still convalescing, he took charge of a school to teach the arts of sabotage, espionage, and paramilitary techniques. Once he recovered, he took command of SS Jagdverband 502, a special operations unit.

In 1943, he and his commandos parachuted into Iran to train mountain tribes in sabotaging Allied supply shipments transported to the Soviet Union on the Trans-Iranian Railway. Skorzeny's fame escalated that September when he led a composite unit of SS commandos and German paratroopers in the daring rescue of deposed Italian fascist dictator Benito Mussolini from his mountain-top prison in the

Apennines. That feat saved Mussolini's life—for a time—and earned Skorzeny a Knight's Cross, Germany's highest military honor. During the Battle of the Bulge the following year, Skorzeny organized Operation Griffin, which sent English-speaking SS commandos behind Allied lines wearing American uniforms to sow confusion and distrust. In February 1944, he was awarded Oak Leaves to go with his Knight's Cross for leading the defense of Schwedt Bridgehead on the River Oder against overwhelming Soviet troops.

Steiner found the SS legend sitting behind a desk in the planning room, dressed in battlefield gray, and enveloped in tobacco smoke as he pored over a variety of maps. Upon entering, he clicked his heels and saluted.

"Ah, Steiner!" Skorzeny said, rising. He came around the desk, his catcher's mitt of a hand outstretched, and grabbed Steiner by the shoulder as he shook his hand. "Steiner, it is good to see you again."

"Good to see you, too, Herr Obersturmbannführer," Steiner said. Skorzeny was not only Steiner's commanding officer, he also served with the senior SS officer during Operation Griffin and in the defense of the Schwedt Bridgehead.

Skorzeny patted Steiner's shoulder and watched as a small cloud of dust appeared. He studied his junior officer, then said, "You look like hell warmed over, Hans. Come, let's have a drink." Skorzeny produced two glasses and a bottle of schnapps from a desk drawer and poured each a full measure. Handing one to Steiner, he toasted, "Salut!"

"To victory," Steiner said.

"Yes. Yes, to victory," Skorzeny said, taking another drink. He opened a box on the desk. "Cigarette? They're Russian."

"Thank you." Steiner took one and bent two crimps into the cardboard mouthpiece the Russian way.

"How is Franz?"

"He is as well as can be expected, considering, Herr Obersturmbannführer."

"In other words, he looks like hell warmed over, too." Steiner nodded.

Skorzeny studied his junior officer awhile before asking, "So, you have spoken to the reichsführer, yes?" Steiner nodded again. "And what do you think of your mission?" When the younger officer hesitated, he added, "Come, come, you may speak freely here."

"All I know of my mission so far, Herr Obersturmbannführer, is I am to cross behind enemy lines to retrieve an ancient relic that some believe to hold mystical powers," Steiner said.

Skorzeny let loose a full belly laugh. "Yes, that is it in a nutshell, isn't it?" he said. "And how do you feel about this mission?"

Steiner sipped his schnapps as he pondered the question. "How does the old English poem go? 'Ours is not to reason why. Ours is but to do or die'."

The Obersturmbannführer nodded. "Tennyson," he said. "But it actually reads, 'Theirs not to reason why. Theirs but to do and die.' But you are correct, ours is not to reason why. We follow orders—the Führer's orders. And if the Führer insists he needs his …" Skorzeny searched for a word.

"Talisman?" Steiner offered.

"Very good. Talisman," Skorzeny said, nodding. "If the Fuhrer insists he needs his talisman, then we must procure it for him—or die trying."

"Where, if I may ask, is the relic?" Steiner asked.

Skorzeny lit another Russian cigarette, waved the thick, gray smoke away from his face, and beckoned Steiner to follow him to a wall map. He placed a meaty finger on the map. "I assume you know this place?"

Steiner studied the map and nodded. "Yes, I have been there."

"Haven't we all?" Skorzeny said. "In the basement, there is a large safe. That's where you will find it."

"May I ask why it was not removed during the retreat?"

"Another officer was detailed to do just that, as well as to destroy the site," Skorzeny said. "He failed to do either.

All he managed to do was set the place on fire. Now we have to rely on you and your men."

"Why us, if I may ask?"

"Because you and most of your men speak English," Skorzeny said.

Steiner's heart dropped. "English?"

"And you are veterans of Operation Griffin."

Steiner's heart dropped even further. "You want us to go behind American lines dressed in their uniforms to get this … this spearhead?"

"Yes," Skorzeny said.

"With all due respect, Herr Obersturmbannführer, but Griffin was not particularly successful. I lost several men."

Skorzeny clasped his hands behind his back and raised his chin. "You are wrong, Hans," he said. "Griffin was spectacularly successful. Too successful, in fact. You and the others spread so much confusion and distrust among the Amis, they began to suspect everybody. That is why we failed in our objective."

Steiner didn't see it that way, but he replied, "If you say so, Herr Obersturmbannführer."

"I do," Skorzeny said. "So, this time you will avoid sowing any confusion or distrust. You must avoid interacting with the Amis at all costs. Simply slip in and slip out."

"And if we can't avoid the Amis?"

"Bluff your way through," Skorzeny said. "Barring that, make certain no one can raise the alarm."

Steiner thought it over. It was possible, he thought, but he still didn't like it. "Two of my men were summarily shot as spies," he said. "That's no way for a soldier to die."

Skorzeny looked at the floor and nodded. "I know," he said.

"Then how can you ask us to do it again?"

Skorzeny sighed, smoke trailing from his nostrils. "You know the answer to that already, Hans," he said.

Steiner studied his senior officer before understanding what he meant. "Ours is not to reason why," he said.

Skorzeny simply nodded.

☼

"I don't like this at all, Hans," Rockenhäuser muttered. "To send us back across the Ami lines in their uniforms. It's … it's unconscionable."

"I know, Franz, I know," Steiner agreed.

Steiner and his second-in-command were driving toward a SS supply depot located outside Tempelhof Airport deep inside Berlin. Rockenhäuser drove the staff car, while Steiner sat in the passenger seat.

They watched a transport plane take off from the airport. "Maybe we should jump on one of those planes and fly to Spain like so many other good party members," Rockenhäuser sneered.

"You're getting reckless in your old age, Franz," Steiner said. "Some parties might consider that statement treasonous."

Rockenhäuser snorted. "What difference would it make? We go on this mission, we're all likely to be shot as spies anyway, like Klinger and Hausmann in Griffin," he said.

"Perhaps," Steiner concurred. "I did bring that up with Skorzeny. He agreed we could wear our uniform tunics under the Ami uniforms. Technically, we'd still be in our uniforms and so the Amis cannot consider us spies."

"Do you truly believe the Amis will make that distinction?"

"Probably not," Steiner said. "We wouldn't." He lit a cigarette and watched the wind snatch away the smoke.

"So why did you agree to this mission, Hans?"

"Blame the English poet Tennyson," Steiner said. "Something about not needing to understand why you're being ordered to do something, you just do it."

"Bloody Tommies," Rockenhäuser cursed. "Didn't they also say something about taking the king's money?"

"If you take the king's penny, you do the king's work," Steiner recited.

"Bloody mercenaries," Rockenhäuser cursed again.

"What's the difference between a Tommy taking the king's penny and us taking the Führer's Reichsmark?"

Rockenhäuser eyed his commanding officer. "You're getting reckless in your old age, Hans," he said, repeating Steiner's own words to him. "Some parties might consider that statement treasonous."

Steiner glanced at his subordinate and chuckled, remembering the near traitorous candor Himmler displayed about losing the war. The chuckle became a full-throated laugh, so void of Steiner's usual wartime weariness Rockenhäuser found it contagious. By the time they reached the supply depot, they were both laughing uproariously.

Chapter 18

MEMBERS OF THE PARSIFAL TEAM were not laughing as they were driven to the Third Army supply depot. The same young soldier who drove Mac to the doorstep of Patton's headquarters outside Frankfurt now drove them to the depot with his same hair-raising, sniper-evading tactics. By the time they arrived at the depot, their knuckles were as white as the clouds floating overhead.

It wasn't just the rough ride that gave them sour moods. Neither Mac nor Roy was happy that Harry's theoretical lure of the spear being hidden in Hitler's personal residence had been bitten on and swallowed by Patton. The morning after Harry suggested they might find the spear in the Berghof, Colonel Fender returned bearing orders personally signed by the general, instructing them to transport themselves to Berchtesgaden "by any means necessary" and search the Berghof for any evidence of the "Imperial Regalia or pieces thereof or any items of which Lieutenant Herschel considered of historical importance."

Mac snorted when he read that line. "It's a goddamn fishing expedition for antiques," he said.

The next sentence, however, truly set Mac's teeth on edge. "Should no such relic(s) be discovered, you are ordered to continue your search anywhere and everywhere Lieutenant Herschel, in his professional capacity, may deem a possible location for any or all pieces of the Imperial Regalia."

"Open-ended orders," Roy muttered. "Great."

"What's that mean?" Harry asked. "Open-ended?"

"Patton doesn't want to be bothered writing additional orders if we find nothing at the Berghof," Mac told him. "But he wants us to keep looking come hell or high water."

"And for the rest of time," Roy added.

Harry still didn't understand their concern. "Well," he said, "I don't have any more ideas where the damn spear might be. So, we take a nice leisurely drive through the countryside up to Berchtesgaden and enjoy some fresh mountain air. If we don't find it, we come back here."

Mac and Roy stared at him. "What?" he asked.

"*Werwölfe*," Mac said.

"Werewolves?" Harry had seen the 1941 movie, *The Wolf Man*, starring the "man of a thousand faces" Lon Chaney as a man who turns into a wolfish monster at each full moon, but he didn't see any connection with their mission. He laughed. "You think there are wolf men running around the Alps?"

"No," Mac said, "SS Werwölfe. Guerilla bands organized by the SS to harass and kill Allied troops and anyone who cooperates with them."

"Basically, the same mission Mac and I had in France with the Jedburghs," Roy added.

"Intelligence has been receiving reports for months of a Nazi plan to continue the war. Hitler calls it the National Redoubt. One method is the use of resistance fighters in the same manner the resistance movements did in German-occupied areas," Mac continued. "They call themselves the Werwölfe after some kind of 17th century guerilla band, or something."

"Yeah, it's also called the Alpine Redoubt because it's all centered around the Bavarian Alps," Roy said. "Right where we're going."

Harry now understood their concern. Their journey to Hitler's Alpine home could lead them directly into a nest of SS Werwölfe. "These werewolves," he asked, "are they very dangerous?"

Mac nodded toward Roy. "We were," he said.

The name of the master sergeant in charge of the supply tent was Patterson, and he greeted them with a curt nod. "What can I do for you gentlemen today, sirs?" he asked with a cornpone drawl.

Mac handed him a requisition form listing all the supplies they needed for the trip to Berchtesgaden, along with a copy of their orders. Patterson glanced over the list, shaking his head, then gave them a wary look. "You all expectin' to take on the German army by yerselves?"

"Something like that," Mac said. "Is there a problem, master sergeant?"

"This here's a lot of equipment for just three GIs," Patterson said.

"Please read our orders, master sergeant," Mac said.

Patterson glanced at the first line of the orders. "O-S-S," he said. "What the hell is that?"

"Office of Strategic Services," Harry explained.

The master sergeant brightened. "Oh, you're one of them entertainer groups that go 'round puttin' on shows for the troops."

"That's *special* services," Mac said.

"Then what are you?"

"We're spies," Roy said.

"Whose side?" Patterson asked.

"Ours," replied Mac.

"Is that the same as my side?" the supply sergeant asked.

"Depends," said Roy. "Whose side are you on?"

Patterson grinned. "You're a funny man. Sure you ain't no entertainer?"

"Master sergeant, would you please look at who signed our orders," Mac said.

Patterson glanced through the rest of the orders until he came to Patton's signature. "Oh, ol' Blood and Guts hisself," he said. "You going on one of his expeditions?"

Mac shook his head. "Sorry?"

"No problem," the sergeant said. "We all knows about the general's expeditions looking for booty and souvenirs. I once traded a Joe a dozen real, fresh eggs we bought from a farmer for a sweet lookin' SS officer's dagger and presented it to the general myself." He nodded and grinned. "Always good to stay on his good side, you know."

"Fine," Mac said, nodding. "Now you know. Can we move on with the supply list?"

"Sure, sure, captain." The sergeant shuffled the papers and looked through the requisition form. "Let's see. One jeep with rear-mounted machine gun." He grunted while shaking his head. "Can't help you there. I can give you a jeep, but ain't got no rear mounts for the .30 cals. I can mount you one for the passenger seat, but even that will be jury-rigged."

"That'll do," Mac said.

"Three Thompsons, five magazines a piece, and one hundred and eighty rounds each." The master sergeant frowned again. "Can't help you there, neither."

"Why not?" Mac asked.

"Well, for one thing, you two is officers," Patterson said, nodding at Mac and Harry. "You're rated for M-1 carbines, not submachine guns."

"Look again, master sergeant. That requisition is also signed by General Patton," Mac said, his voice tight.

Patterson skipped to the bottom of the form. "Well, looky there, it sure is. Still can't give you no Tommy guns, though."

"And why is that?" Mac's voice tightened more.

"Ain't got any, captain," the master sergeant said. "All they's sending us these days is Greasers."

"Greasers?" asked Harry.

"Yes, sir, grease guns, ya know?" Patterson answered.

Harry looked at Mac and Roy. "M-3 submachine guns," Mac said. "Replacement for the Tommy." Mac turned to the supply sergeant. "That's fine, master sergeant."

"Okay," the supply sergeant said, making a check mark on the requisition form. He whistled as he read on. "Plastic explosives and detonators. Check. C-rations. Check. K-rat—boy, captain, this is a whole lot of rats for just the three of you."

"Where we're going, we may need to *elicit* information from the local population," Mac explained. "Right now, food—even rations—is more valuable than money."

"Hoowee, you sure right about that, sir," Patterson said. "You'd make a damn fine supply sergeant, you know that, captain?"

"Thank you, master sergeant," Mac said. "I'll take that as a compliment."

"You don't have any silk stockings, do you?" asked Roy, grinning.

The sergeant squinted at Roy. "Sure do, but I'm wearing them."

Roy held up his hands. "Never mind."

"Now, how soon can we get our supplies, master sergeant?" Mac asked.

Glancing at the remaining items, Patterson said, "Take a couple of hours to get the jeep and mount the .30, gas her up. Rest of this stuff don't take long. Say three hours?"

"Good." Mac nodded. He thought of something. "Oh, do you have a big box you could somehow mount on the back of the jeep? To keep all this stuff in. Be great if it locked, too."

Patterson thought it over a moment. "I could bolt a foot-locker on the back," he said. "You'd have to tie the spare to your hood and keep the gas can in the back seat."

"That's fine," Mac said.

"You'll need to supply your own lock for the foot-locker," the sergeant said. "We ain't got none 'cept for the ones locking our supply cages."

"I'll find one, Ma—er, sir," Roy said.

Mac glanced at his wristwatch. "Good. Then we'll be back in three hours."

As the three turned to walk out of the tent, the supply sergeant yelled, "Happy hunting!" After a brief chuckle, he muttered to himself, "That general sure do love his old stuff."

Chapter 19

STEINER SIGNALED FOR HIS small convoy to stop. The SS commando officer had requisitioned two captured American 2.5-ton trucks and a Willys scout car, which the Amis referred to as a jeep. Each truck carried eight of Steiner's men while Steiner rode in the jeep with Rockenhäuser driving. Each vehicle bore the Wehrmacht's Balkenkreuz, or bar cross, painted on an olive-green square of canvas secured to the doors; Steiner didn't want their own troops to shoot at them as they crossed into the American lines.

They had found their way across through a narrow gap Skorzeny identified in the western lines. Now they were behind the American lines, it was time to assume their disguise. Steiner climbed out of the jeep, removed his field cap, and unbuttoned his outer SS jacket. Beneath it was his SS tunic, though the trousers and boots he wore were American GI-issued. He pulled an American combat jacket and helmet from a captured GI rucksack, slipped them on, then stuffed his SS jacket and field cap into the ruck. Rockenhäuser and the other men followed suit as Steiner walked around the vehicles, ripping off the Balkenkreuz. Beneath each cross was a white five-pointed American star.

Steiner approached a Scharführer. "Staff sergeant," he said in English, "have the men fall in for a quick inspection. Look for anything that doesn't look American."

"Jawohl, Herr Sturmbannführer!"

"Speak English!"

"Yes, sir," the chastened noncom replied.

The commandos piled out of the trucks and formed up in three ranks of six men each. Steiner and Rockenhäuser walked between the ranks examining each man, fixing a collar here, a pocket there, making sure nothing of their SS tunics beneath the combat jackets protruded. Satisfied, Steiner faced the formation, Rockenhäuser at his side.

"From now on, we speak nothing but English," he said. "We speak English. We think English. We shit English." A murmur of laughter came from the men. "If you need to curse, curse in English. If you are wounded, scream in pain in English. We do not want the Amis to know we are here. Do you understand?"

"Yes, sir!" came the response in chorus.

A hand went up in the formation. Steiner nodded toward the soldier. "Yes, what is it?"

"Do you know any good American swear words, sir?"

Steiner smiled as the disguised soldiers chuckled. "Perhaps Staff Sergeant Blösch knows a few?" he said, turning to the Scharführer.

Blösch nodded. "As you know, I lived in America for several years. The most widely used swear word is fuck. Americans believe everything has a sex life, so it's 'fucking this' and 'fucking that.' Just fuck everything and everyone."

More laughter.

"Very instructive, staff sergeant," Steiner said. "A lesson well learned. Now, mount up!"

Steiner turned toward his jeep when the staff sergeant stopped him. "Major, not all our men speak fluent English."

"I'm aware of that," Steiner said. "Tell them to avoid speaking at all, especially if we encounter any Yanks."

"Yes, sir," the sergeant said. He turned and trotted toward the trucks. "You heard the man. Mount up!"

They drove for half an hour before encountering their first Americans. Four MPs led by a corporal manned a road block. A thin log held up by sawhorses stretched across the road. The corporal carried an M-3 grease gun, and the privates M-1 Garands. They seemed surprised to see American vehicles coming toward them from the east. The corporal readied his weapon and held up a hand.

Steiner's jeep rolled up alongside the corporal, and Steiner climbed out.

"Hoowee, corporal," he said. "Are we glad to see you!"

Still confused, the corporal asked, "Major, where the hell are you coming from? Those are the German lines over there. We're here to prevent anyone from going further east."

"Hell, corporal, don't we know that! We just come from behind the jerry lines," Steiner said, waving a map taken from a captured American officer. "We come up here looking for the front last night and got our damn asses lost. Next thing we hear krauts talking. One of my men—he's a good kid—his folks come from the old country, so he speaks some kraut. He tells me we crossed the lines. Damn! Double damn! So's we just turn our asses around and come back the way we went. Damn, I'm glad to see you, corporal. You look so damn pretty, I could kiss you!"

The corporal still looked confused. He glanced at Rockenhäuser, who smiled back at him. "Our CO is pretty demonstrative," he said.

"Yeah, what he said," Steiner said. He waved the map again. "Now can y'all tell me how to get ourselves to brigade?"

As the corporal and Steiner studied the map, an MP private walked along the convoy, smiling and nodding at the soldiers looking down at him. He stopped at the back of the second truck and lit a cigarette. A glint from one of the soldier's boots caught his attention—sunlight reflecting off the silver pommel of a German dagger.

"Whoa, is that an SS dagger?" he asked.

The commando with the knife stared wide-eyed at the MP but said nothing.

"Well, is it?"

The German soldier nodded but stayed silent.

The commando sitting opposite the man with the dagger thought fast. "Smith here has a terrible cold and laryngitis," he said, Anglicizing his comrade's German name Schmidt. "It hurts him to talk."

Schmidt coughed a couple of times.

"Can I see it?"

"Let him see it, Smith," the second soldier urged.

The SS commando drew the dagger from his boot and handed it to the MP, who studied it in the sunlight. "Damn, that's a beauty," he said. "Where'd you get it?" He looked at the soldier he knew as Smith. "Take it off a dead kraut?"

Schmidt coughed two more times.

"Nah, he's just up from the repo depot," said the second SS soldier. "Probably bought it off someone back there. Goes around wearing it in his boot like some damn Hollywood commando." He shrugged. "Replacements, what you gonna do?"

"Hey, I got some poker winnings," the MP told Smith/Schmidt. "You want to sell it?"

The German shook his head. His friend spoke for him. "He wants to send it back to his girlfriend, make himself look like a genuine war hero to her, you know?"

The MP frowned and shook his head as he handed the dagger back. "Too bad," he said. "Won't mind sending one of those back to my old man, make him think I'm a hero. Be the first time he thought kind of me." He reached into his pocket and pulled out a wad of money, holding it up as if tempting the German. "Sure you don't want to sell it?"

"I told you—"

"Let the man speak for himself," the MP said. "Laryngitis or no laryngitis, he can say yes or no, can't he?" He stared at the commando with the knife. "Well?"

Schmidt stared at the GI, his mouth working nervously. Then cautiously he said, "Fuck?"

The MP stuck the money back in his pocket. "Well, you don't have to get goddam nasty about it." He turned and stormed back to the roadblock.

Steiner thanked the MP corporal, who then lifted one end of the log and moved it aside to let the convoy pass. Rockenhäuser put the jeep in first gear as Steiner settled into his seat. He stole a quick glance at the MPs. What he saw made him take the jeep out of gear. "Hans," he whispered, cocking his head toward the GIs.

Turning, Steiner saw one of the MPs speaking quickly and urgently to the corporal and pointing over his shoulder toward the back of the last truck. Steiner climbed out of the jeep and pulled his M-1 carbine from the rifle holster strapped to the right front fender. He glanced at the MPs again, then glanced back at his convoy. Blösch looked back at him from the passenger seat of the first truck. Steiner nodded.

"Hey, major," the MP corporal called out as he stomped back toward the jeep.

Steiner swung the barrel of his carbine up and shot the corporal in the chest. Blösch leapt from his truck with a Thompson and fired several short bursts at the remaining MPs. They all went down. The SS sergeant then quick marched to the fallen GIs and fired a single coup de grâce into each body.

Steiner approached the Scharführer. "What happened?" he demanded.

"Schmidt left his dagger stuffed in the top of his boot," Blösch said. "The American wanted to buy it from him, but Schmidt is one of our men whose English isn't very good."

Steiner cursed. "The idiot!" Forcing himself not to run, the SS officer strode along the convoy, stopping at the tail gate of the second truck. "Schmidt, fall in!"

Schmidt climbed down from the truck and stood at attention before Steiner.

Steiner held out his hand. "Give it to me."

The young soldier swallowed hard, leaned down and removed the dagger, then handed it to Steiner hilt first.

"You were ordered to remove or hide anything that indicated you were German," Steiner said.

"Yes, sir," Schmidt said in heavily accented English.

"You admit disobeying my order?"

"Ye—no, sir," Schmidt stammered. "I—I forgot about the knife, sir."

"You forgot about it?" The young SS soldier nodded, his eyes wide with fear. "How do you forget about something like this—" He waved the dagger in Schmidt's face. "After being clearly ordered to dispose of or hide anything that could betray us?" Steiner faced the soldiers in the truck. "How could any of you let this happen after receiving such orders?"

The crestfallen SS commandos' heads drooped, their eyes staring at the truck bed. Steiner turned his attention back to Schmidt.

"You forgot," he said, "and your forgetfulness betrayed us to the enemy. Your forgetfulness nearly ended this mission before it began. You are never going to forget again."

Steiner thrust the dagger into the youth's chest, twisting it left and right to slice through the major arteries and heart. The commando dropped and didn't move. Steiner addressed the men in the trucks again.

"I order you again," he said, "to check each other and make certain there is nothing showing that can betray who we are. And make certain each man sitting near the tail gate can speak English."

The soldiers stood and began checking each other's uniforms. Steiner nodded to the dead SS commando.

"Blösch, take him into the tree line and cover him with leaves," he said. "If we're lucky, no one will find him until we finish this mission."

<h1 style="text-align:center">Chapter 20</h1>

A THICK, GRAY CLOUD of tobacco smoke encircled Kazimir Stanislav as he sat at his desk in Stavka headquarters in Moscow. Stavka was the primary command center of the Soviet Army. As assistant chief of the army's special purpose forces, Stanislav's job was to organize, brief, and dispatch the army's commando units on their missions. The operation he was organizing just then was not one he agreed with, but that meant little to his superiors. He learned long ago to disagree with or oppose the army hierarchy rarely resulted in anything less than a long vacation in a Siberian gulag or, worse, a firing squad.

Stanislav smashed out his cigarette and took another from a box on his desk, crimping the cardboard holder twice. The epaulets of his brown officer's jacket bore the four bars and crossed rifles of a *polkóvnik*, or colonel. He stood, stretched, then searched the pockets of his tan cavalry pants for his lighter before remembering he had placed it in his desk drawer. Retrieving the lighter, he lit the cigarette and filled the room with more smoke. Then he sat again, and for the umpteenth time rubbed his jackbooted feet while cursing the army's one-size-fits-all footwear policy.

Someone rapped smartly on his office door. Stanislav lowered his foot. "Come!"

His mood brightened when Captain Valentin Valery entered the office. Valery was the physical opposite of Stanislav. Where the colonel was short and thick, Valery was tall and muscular. Stanislav's face was flat and jowly, with deep set dark eyes topped by a thick, bushy unibrow. Valery's face was thin and handsome, with an aquiline nose and youthful blue eyes, though—Stanislav noticed—the eyes had lost some of their youthfulness since the last time he saw him.

The colonel rose as Valery marched up to his desk and saluted. "Captain Valentin Valery, reporting as ordered, Comrade Colonel."

Stanislav returned the salute, then came around the desk and took Valery by the shoulders. "Valya!" he said, using the diminutive of Valery's given name. "It's been months!"

"Four months in a hospital, Comrade Colonel," Valery said. "Each day like a stay in a gulag. I am glad to be out."

The senior officer looked Valery over. "You are fully convalesced? You are healthy?"

Valery nodded. "And ready to return to duty."

"Good! Good! Here sit. Sit." Stanislav waved the younger officer into a guest chair. He reached for the cigarette box and held it out to Valery. "Cigarette?"

"Thank you, no," Valery said. He tapped his left chest where a German sniper bullet had punctured his lung. "The doctors tell me it would not be good for the lung."

"Of course," Stanislav said, putting out his own cigarette and making a vain attempt to wave the smoke away from his desk. He reached into a drawer and pulled out a bottle of vodka and two glasses. "This would not hurt your lung, am I correct?"

Valery smiled. "You are correct, Comrade Colonel."

Stanislav poured two full glasses, passed one to the captain, then raised his and made the traditional toast. "K Stalinu!" *To Stalin!*

"K Stalinu!" repeated Valery, and they both downed their drinks.

The colonel refilled their glasses. "To comrades now gone!"

"To comrades now gone!"

Another refill, and Stanislav toasted, "May no one ever drink the last toast for those of us here!"

With the ceremonial toasts completed, Stanislav belched and put the bottle and glasses back into their drawer. He reached for a cigarette, but thought better of it.

"Please, Comrade Colonel, please indulge," Valery said. "If I cannot smoke for myself, I can still appreciate someone else's tobacco smoke."

Stanislav smiled, took a cigarette, crimped the holder, and lit it. After taking a deep, satisfying drag, he said, "Now, let us get down to the matter at hand." He picked up a folder and handed it to Valery. "Are you familiar with the decadent Christian mythology surrounding the so-called Spear of Destiny?"

Valery opened the folder, finding a photograph of the Longinus lance head. He frowned and shook his head. There were no churches in the atheistic Soviet Union to teach Christian mythology. "Only what I have read in English Literature about King Arthur and the Knights of the Round Table."

The older man smiled and wagged a finger at Valery. The two men were as intellectually opposite as they were physically. Stanislav came from a *kolkhoz,* or farming collective, the descendant of hard-working but unworldly peasant stock. Valery's father was a diplomat stationed at the Soviet embassy in London. Valya attended British schools and grew up rubbing shoulders with the English aristocracy. The colonel was gruff, often vulgar, while the young captain was sophisticated and erudite. And yet Stanislav was quite fond of Valery, and not just because he was a fine soldier. Stanislav saw in the younger officer a version of his one and only son, who was killed in the early fighting when Germany invaded the Motherland.

"Ah, yes, I forgot you were studying literature before the war. You're going to be the next Tolstoy."

Blushing, Valery said, "If I survive long enough."

"You remember to put me in one of your books," the colonel said. "Make me a hero."

"But you are a hero, Comrade Colonel."

"I am an old man who sits behind a desk," Stanislav said, "shuffling through papers. My war is fought up there." He pointed to the ceiling toward the offices of his superiors. "And I am losing my war."

Valery said nothing.

Stanislav moved on. "Right. This myth that whoever owns the spear will become a great leader has caught Comrade Stalin's attention. That scourge Hitler stole it from a museum in Vienna for himself. Apparently, he believes in such nonsense. We have developed intelligence that the spear has become … misplaced. We also learned that both the SS and the American OSS have launched operations to retrieve the spear." He looked at a file on his desk. "An American captain named MacAuley and a Waffen SS major named Steiner." He handed a folder to the captain. "Here is some information on both of them."

"Interesting," Valery said, "But what do we care?"

"Comrade Stalin wants you to retrieve the spear before they do."

One of Valery's eyebrows shot up. "May I ask why Comrade Stalin would care about a Christian relic?"

"If Hitler believes the spear is his personal talisman, then Comrade Stalin wants to deprive him of it."

"And why deprive the Americans of it?" Valery asked.

Stanislav sat back and hesitated before speaking. "Sometimes, Valya, you ask questions you shouldn't ask." He took a deep breath, then said, "Comrade Stalin believes his possession of this religious icon would be a significant propaganda victory. He believes with this ... trinket ... in his possession, those western countries which believe in its power would fall before us and we could spread the ... *benefits* ... of communism throughout the west."

"And he would become the next great leader in the myth," Valery said.

The colonel pounded the desk top but held back his anger. "Valya, your mouth has lost some of its control. Is that a normal symptom of being shot in the chest?"

"If it is, Comrade Colonel, the doctors did not mention it," Valery said. "May I ask how you obtained such intelligence?"

"We have a mole in Himmler's office," Stanislav said in a lower voice.

"And the American OSS as well?"

Stanislav nodded. "But that never leaves here, understand?"

"Yes, Comrade Colonel," Valery said. He took the chance to change the subject. "Where am I to find this spear?"

"Come here." Stanislav rose from his desk and stepped over to a wall map. Slipping on a pair of reading glasses, he searched the map until he found what he was looking for. "According to our German agent, right here," he said, removing the glasses and using them to point to the spot. "The SS was ordered to retrieve it before the Germans retreated, but they failed. Now they are sending another SS unit to retrieve it."

Valery studied the map, tracing the lines showing the western front. "That's inside the American lines. How do I get there?"

"There is a military delegation flying from here to Eisenhower's headquarters in London," Stanislav said. "They will fly in two Lisunov Li-2s. You and a dozen of your parachute-trained *spetsnaz* will also be on board." The colonel used the shortened version of *voyska spetsial'nogo naznacheniya,* or special purpose troops. "They will fly a route over the lines that will take you near your target." He tapped the map with his glasses. "Here. About ten kilometers from the target. After landing, you and your men will route march to the target."

"And what of German fighters?" Valery asked.

"The Luftwaffe is broken, Valya," the colonel said. "And you will be flying at night. There should be no encounters with German aircraft and the Americans are expecting our delegation."

"Once we have the spear, how do we return to our lines?"

"By whatever means necessary," Stanislav said. "Route march back if you have to. Or find some convenient transportation. If necessary, turn yourselves over to the Americans. Say you inadvertently crossed through German lines and ask them to repatriate you. Our troops are already close to linking up with theirs at the Elbe River near Torgau. Here." He placed a meaty finger on the map. "I suspect they will greet you with smiles and hugs."

As Valery scrutinized the map, various tactical options flitted through his mind. Finally, he nodded. "When do we leave?"

"Tonight," Stanislav said. He stepped back around his desk and pulled out the vodka and glasses again. "But first, another toast!"

Chapter 21

TWO LISUNOV LI-2S TOOK off that night from an air-field outside of Moscow. Each carried half of the four-man liaison team headed to meet with Eisenhower's staff, and a dozen Spetsnaz parachutists. Two Yak-3 fighters flew above them as escorts. The round-about route needed to take Valery and his men over the drop zone near their target would require a refueling stop in France before the quick hop across the English Channel. By then, the parachutists would no longer be on board.

Valery stood near the open cargo door of one Li-2, staring out at the night sky. For the most part, his thoughts were about the details of the mission, but every few minutes they were interrupted by what he considered a great irony. The Lisunov Li-2 was the Soviet version of the Douglas C-47 cargo and transport plane the British called the Dakota and the Americans referred to as the Gooney Bird. The Russians had been building the aircraft under license from the Americans since the late 1930s.

How like the capitalist Americans to sell their technology to a communist country opposed to the very existence of capitalism. But that, he knew, was the great self-defeating vice of capitalism—greed. The Americans would sell their technology and skills to anyone for a price. Did they not help finance and build Nazi Germany's war machine? Only fourteen years after forcing a defeated Germany into economic ruin, the Americans came with their manufacturing ingenuity to help build Hitler's grandiose dream of a thousand-year Reich. That maniac even presented medals to the Americans' vaunted automaker Henry Ford for his support in rearming the Nazi military forces. Then Hitler declared war on the U.S.

Another thought, just as ironic, forced its way into Valery's head. The Soviet Union had done as much as the Americans, perhaps even more. Since the late 1920s, the USSR secretly assisted Germany in rebuilding its military, a violation of the Versailles Treaty. The Russians trained German army officers and aviators, and helped them design and test new military planes and tanks. Ah! Valery told himself. But Russia learned much about air and tank warfare and military leadership from the Germans. It was mutually beneficial. What did the Americans get other than a bigger profit margin for their richest capitalists?

Valery sighed. His thinking was going in circles. And he was thinking things he should not think—always a problem with him. How did Stanislav put it? *Sometimes, Valya, you ask questions you shouldn't ask.*

Flashes of light grabbed Valery's attention. Tracers arched through the dark, seeming to come from nowhere.

He watched them slam into the other Li-2 and within seconds, the cargo plane disappeared in a massive fireball.

"Enemy fighter!" he screamed, as bullets punched through the thin aluminum skin of his aircraft.

He saw several of his men thrown out of their seats as the machine gun fire riddled their bodies. One of the delegation members repeatedly screamed, "Where are our escorts? Where are our escorts?" until another burst of gunfire took off his head.

Outside the cargo door, Valery saw exhaust flames from a fighter streak past. Ours or theirs? he wondered. Seconds later, the port engine caught fire. He glanced forward, saw the remaining delegate struggling to strap on a parachute. Beyond him, one of the pilots leaned out of the cockpit, screaming something Valery couldn't hear but understood just the same. He turned to his men, jerking both thumbs upward and yelling, "Get up! Get up! Hook up and jump."

The remaining Spetsnaz leapt up, hooked their static cords to an overhead cable, and scrambled toward the cargo door. Valery rushed them out of the burning Lisunov, callously throwing anyone who stumbled out of the hatch. Another round of fire struck the plane. Valery saw it strike the remaining delegate and an aircrewman. Both pilots hung lifeless in their seatbelts. Turning, he hurled himself out the door into the night.

In the dark, he seemed to hover in mid-air with no sense of falling. Then the static line pulled tight, and he heard the rustle of the pilot chute rushing out of its pack, tugging the main chute along with it. He felt his leg straps cinch into his groin as the main chute blossomed. He looked up and, in the distance, watched as the burning cargo plane spiraled toward the ground.

Stanislav's words came to him again. *The Luftwaffe is broken, Valya.*

It was morning by the time the surviving parachutists came together on the ground. There had been twenty-four Spetsnaz soldiers in the two planes. Now there were only eight. Twelve died when the first Li-2 exploded. Four in Valery's stick either died inside the cargo plane from gunfire or were killed in the jump. The survivors sat on the ground in small circles, not talking, still in shock.

Valery stood apart, studying a topographical map, a compass in one hand. Occasionally, he looked up, trying to distinguish some landmark he could identify on the map. He spotted a soldier emerging from the tall grass surrounding them and hailed him. "Serzhánt Alexeyev!"

The sergeant trotted toward him, stopped, and saluted. "Comrade Captain?"

"Any luck?"

"No, sir," Alexeyev said. "No bodies, no unaccounted-for parachutes. It looks like they died in the plane."

Valery nodded and frowned.

"Any idea where we are, sir?"

Valery puffed up his cheeks and blew air through pursed lips. He pointed to a spot on the map. "This is the landing zone we were heading for, but we had to jump maybe fifteen minutes early. I estimate we're somewhere around here." He pointed to another map point.

"That looks like twenty, perhaps thirty kilometers from our target," the sergeant said.

"At least thirty," the captain said. "We find this road to the west of us, it should take us to there."

"A lot of that is uphill," Alexeyev said. "That will slow us down."

Valery nodded and looked at his watch. "Which means we need to get started now. Get them up, sergeant."

Chapter 22

THE IMMENSE ASPHALT RIBBON the Germans called the Reichsautobahn snaked through the Bavarian Alps, climbing toward the alpine village of Berchtesgaden. Despite its size—far bigger than any highway Harry and the others ever saw in the States—Allied vehicles crammed the autobahn. Tanks, halftracks, trucks, and jeeps crept south bumper-to-bumper toward Bavaria, filling both lanes as the road climbed up the Alps. Semi-hidden in the bordering trees were German planes—some damaged or destroyed, some as yet untouched—which once used the "autobahn" as an improvised airfield.

Roy wove the jeep around and through the slow traffic and past a long column of sour-looking German prisoners of war being marched northward toward the rear. The higher they got, the cooler the air despite it being a pleasantly sunny early morning. One-by-one, Roy, Mac, and Harry donned their combat jackets, zipped them up, and turned up the collars.

"I still don't get it," Roy said. "Hitler's dead. Why are we still chasing this spear thing?"

The day before, German radio announced the death of Adolf Hitler. Joseph Goebbels' propaganda machine claimed the Führer died "defending the Fatherland" in Berlin, but foreign news agencies reported he died by his own hand in his underground bunker. The German army in the west was surrendering in droves, but officially the war was not yet over.

"Because Patton still wants it," Mac said.

Colonel Fender gave them the bad news before they left Patton's new headquarters in Frankfurt. "Sorry, boys, the mission's still on. The general wants the spear before—and I quote—'the goddam commie Rooskies get it and rain hellfire down on us'."

"I swear, Patton—probably Fender, too—saw us coming," Mac griped. "They probably consider us pure fools."

Harry chuckled. "Well, we are," he said, and chuckled again.

"What's that supposed to mean?" Mac demanded.

"Parsifal," Harry said. "According to the story, only a fool with a pure heart could find the spear and the Holy Grail. Wagner renamed his hero from Percival to Parsifal because in Persian it means *pure fool*."

Mac and Roy glanced at each other, shaking their heads. Then Roy snickered and Mac chuckled, and all three broke into uproarious laughter.

Occasionally, they were stopped by MPs manning turnoffs and guiding some vehicles off the autobahn toward where their orders directed them. Usually, a quick glance at Patton's orders and the MPs would wave the three on. Usually.

"Sorry, captain, still can't let you go on, orders or no orders from Ol' Blood and Guts," an MP sergeant said at a roadblock just outside Munich.

Mac heard distant gunfire. "What's happening, sergeant?"

"Some of our fellas were ambushed up ahead, a hundred yards or so," the MP explained. "Krauts took out a tank and a coupla trucks with a Panzerfaust. It's them wolf men they warned us about. You know, some kind of radical Nazis don't know the war is over."

"Werwölfe," Mac said.

"Pardon, sir?"

"They call themselves Werwölfe," Mac said. "German for werewolves. And sergeant, the war isn't over yet."

"Perhaps, sir," the sergeant said with a shrug. "Anyways, some GIs are trying to flush them out, but it's pretty open on the other side of the bend and the krauts are dug in. They're waiting for another tank to come up."

"How far ahead did you say the ambush was?" Mac asked.

"Hundred yards or so, as the crow flies." The MP pointed to a ridge that dropped off toward the road. "Just beyond that bend."

Mac studied the wooded hillside a while, then turned to Roy.

"Think you can make this jeep climb up through those trees?"

Roy took his time studying the terrain. He pursed his lips in thought and waggled his head before shrugging. "Probably. What do you have in mind?"

"If we can get over that ridge to the other side of the bend," Mac said, "we could come down behind the ambush."

"What?" Harry said. "Why don't we just wait here?"

"Longer we wait, more likely more of our guys are going to die," Mac said, racking a round into the .30 caliber machine gun. "And the longer it's going to take us to find that damned spearhead."

Roy put the jeep in gear and gunned the engine. The MP jumped back. "What are you doing, captain?"

"We're going to ambush the ambushers," said Roy, grinning.

"It's what we do," Mac said. He shrugged. "It's a living."

"Or a dying," complained Harry, bracing himself as the jeep jumped forward.

Roy sounded his horn as he nosed the jeep toward the center island of the autobahn that the POWs used on their trek north. The German line parted, and he drove onto the other side, still using his horn to make the military traffic there slow down and separate to let him through. The jeep bounced off the asphalt onto the leaf-covered forest floor and climbed up the hillside. Roy drove through the trees as if he was on a slalom course while Harry and Mac held on with both hands. Weaving sharply to avoid the trees, the jeep's wheels slipped on the wet leafy ground cover and side-slipped several feet downhill. Roy cranked the wheel to the left, gave the engine more gas, and the jeep turned its nose back uphill and once again climbed.

"Roy, you been taking driving lessons from that kid who drove us to the supply depot?" Harry shouted.

"No," Roy answered, laughing. "I trained *him*."

The jeep launched over the ridge, landed with a bounce, and Roy braked to a stop. He picked up his grease gun and racked a round into the breach. Harry did the same with his greaser.

The MP sergeant was right about the ambush site. The trees ended a little past the ridgeline, leaving the sloping ground devoid of cover. Mac was impressed; it was a good choice for an ambush, with a clear field of fire that would cut down anyone climbing up to attack the ambushers. The four or five dead American soldiers scattered on the hillside paid somber testament to that.

From their position on the ridgeline, they could see the convoy stretching both to the north and south. Directly below, a Sherman tank and two 2.5-ton trucks sat burning and blocking the road, still smoldering bodies of dead soldiers strewn around them. A squad of GIs sheltered in a ravine where a German machine gun had them trapped. The rapidity of the machine gun bursts identified the gun as an MG-42, what the GIs referred to as Hitler's Zipper because of its unusual sound. Occasionally, a burst of gunfire rose from the convoy, but it was blind fire aimed at nothing in particular.

Mac followed the sound of the MG-42 to his left and spotted the machine gun nestled behind a deposit of boulders. Five men in civilian clothing hunkered together in a trench behind the rocks, two serving the MG-42, one shouldering a Panzerfaust, and two armed with Mauser rifles. Mac pointed out the nest to Roy and Harry.

"Plan?" asked Roy.

Mac shook his head. "If we try to sneak up on them from behind on foot, we're likely to get hit by our own people," he said, frowning. He thought a moment. "I think we run them down with the jeep. Go in firing the .30 and the greasers. The guys trapped in the ravine and on the convoy are likely to recognize the jeep and realize we're the good guys and stop firing."

"How likely is 'likely'?" Harry asked.

"About the same as a hope and a prayer," Roy said.

"You guys have any better ideas?" Mac asked.

Roy and Harry both shook their heads.

Mac grabbed the .30's pistol grip. "All right. Let's go."

Roy put the jeep in gear and nosed it downhill.

It was over in thirty seconds. The Werwölfe heard the approach of the jeep but had little chance to turn their machine gun or the Panzerfaust on it. Mac showered them with a long burst from the .30 caliber, backed up with short bursts from Harry's grease gun. The two German riflemen got off one shot each with their bolt-action Mausers before the automatic fire from the jeep cut them down. Roy braked the jeep and killed the engine, then jumped out with his M-3 and checked each German. They were all dead.

Mac and Harry approached the machine gun nest, their grease guns held ready. Roy searched each body but found nothing but a pack of captured British cigarettes. He looked up at Mac and the team leader knew the sergeant was experiencing the same sense of irony he was.

The tables had turned. A year ago in France, they had been the hunted. Now, *they* were the hunters.

Chapter 23

DESPITE SITTING AT TWENTY-THREE hundred feet elevation, Berchtesgaden is nestled in a basin formed by some of the tallest mountains in the Bavarian Alps. The triple-peaked massif called the Watzmann, Germany's third tallest mountain, rises to the south. The Kehlstein, a sub-peak of the Hoher Göll Massif, straddles the German-Austrian border. At its peak sits the infamous Kehlsteinhaus, or Eagle's Nest, used by Nazi officials for official and social events.

Adolf Hitler began vacationing in Berchtesgaden as far back as the 1920s, long before coming to power. Before the war, it was a popular holiday spot for wealthy Europeans including, ironically, former Prime Minister David Lloyd George, who led Britain to victory over Germany in WWI, and Neville Chamberlain, the pre-war prime minister who only a few years before promised "peace in our time" after meeting with Hitler.

In early 1945, however, there were no vacationers, only occupying GIs and French *soldats*. Roy maneuvered the jeep through narrow streets crammed with tanks, trucks, and other vehicles, and tired soldiers milling about with looted bottles of wine and schnapps, waiting for the war to end. He bleated his horn, urging them out of the way, but the typical response was a one-finger salute.

"Harry, you've been here before?" Mac asked.

Herschel nodded. "Before the war. For the skiing."

"Then you know your way around?"

"Yes, though a lot has changed since the war," Harry said. "But the Berghof isn't down here in Berchtesgaden." He gestured upward with his finger toward the flank of the Hoher Göll. "It's actually up there in Obersalzberg."

Roy continued pushing his way through the crowded streets while Harry supplied uncertain directions. When they finally reached the road leading up the mountain, an MP hopelessly trying to control traffic stopped them. When Mac showed his orders from Patton, the MP shook his head.

"Captain, I'd like to help you get up there, but everyone's acting like tourists," he said. "Everyone wants to see where Hitler lived. All I can do is wish you luck getting there and tell you to be careful. There's a bunch of paratroopers up there, and they ain't taking orders from nobody."

It took over two hours to push through the traffic clogging the mountain road to Obersalzberg. When they arrived, another weary MP directed them to a major. The major was tall and good-looking, and carried himself the way of men who have seen too much combat and aren't quite certain victory was near. He wore jump wings with two combat stars and the Screaming Eagle patch of the 101st Airborne.

"Imperial Regalia?" the major said, reading Patton's orders. "What the hell is that?"

"Relics from the Holy Roman Empire that Hitler stole from a museum in Vienna, sir," Harry said.

"Oh, yeah, I heard there was some kind of unit trying to recover artwork. What do you call yourselves? The Monuments Men?" The major spotted the jump wings on Mac's shirt, then on Roy's and Harry's. "You have to be jump qualified for that kind of work?"

"Different unit, major," Mac said. "We're OSS. Office of Strategic Services."

"What kind of outfit is that?" the major asked.

"Covert operations," Mac said. "Spying."

"You mean like those guys that helped the resistance in France before the invasion?"

"Yes, sir."

"Well, then, we're almost like brothers," the major said, handing back Patton's orders. "We're paratroopers. Like you, we're supposed to be surrounded."

Mac and Roy laughed politely. The major's eyes narrowed, and he asked, "Why send people like you to collect some old relic?"

Mac grimaced. "Take the king's coin, you give the king his due, I guess."

The major pondered that before nodding. "How can I help you?"

"Well, sir," Mac said, "we believe there is an item—one of the relics we're seeking—that Hitler may have kept in the Berghof. We know there was inevitable looting—"

"We call it souvenir hunting, captain."

"Souvenir hunting," Mac continued. "We'd like to address your men and if anyone found it, we'd like to retrieve it … for the general."

The major thought about that, his eyes narrowing. "Suppose one of my men does have this item. You going to cause problems for him? Get him in trouble?"

"Not at all, sir," Mac said. "There's nothing illegal about … souvenir hunting."

Nodding, the major said, "Okay." He hailed a second lieutenant who looked too war weary to be a recent graduate of officer candidate school. Mac guessed a battlefield promotion. "Take these men up to the Eagle's Nest and have Easy fall in. These guys want to address them."

"Eagle's Nest?" asked Harry. "Not the Berghof?"

"The SS set the Berghof on fire before they retreated," the major explained. "Easy Company's been quartering in the SS barracks over there." He gestured to an Alpine-style apartment complex. "When off duty, they spend most of their time in the Eagle's Nest. But if anything was taken from the Berghof, it would've been found by someone in Easy."

The lieutenant hopped into their jeep and directed them farther up the mountain. "How's it feel to be a butter bar, lieutenant?"

The lieutenant gave Mac an embarrassed grin. "That obvious?"

"It's obvious you're not just out of OCS," Mac said. "What were you before the hardware?"

"Platoon sergeant," the lieutenant said. "Promoted after the Ardennes offensive."

"Good for you."

"I don't know," the paratrooper said. "I miss my guys. But we'll be seeing them soon, and I'm sure as hell they're going to give me grief over these bars."

☼

The RAF had not been kind to Obersalzberg. The Nazi Party confiscated much of the town and turned it into a retreat for the party's top echelon. Party secretary Martin Bormann and Luftwaffe chief Hermann Goering both had houses near the Berghof, and the SS built a large barracks to house Hitler's bodyguard. Fearing it might be used as a mountain headquarters for Hitler's long-rumored Alpine Redoubt, more than three hundred Lancaster bombers and Mosquito fighter bombers attacked Obersalzberg only a few days before its liberation by Allied forces. The mountainous terrain bedeviled the bombers. Bombs destroyed the Bormann and Goering homes, as well as part of the SS barracks, but Hitler's residence was only damaged, and the Eagle's Nest was unscathed. The air raid was not considered a success.

Hitler's private retreat survived the bombing, but not the SS's torching. The grand residence which once graced the pages of American and European architectural magazines was now a scorched skeleton. Still, enough remained for GIs to mill around swigging booze liberated from Hitler's cellar and admiring the view of the Bavarian Alps. The lieutenant had Roy stop the jeep, then he stood up and addressed the soldiers.

"Easy, listen up!"

Some soldiers whistled or gave cat calls to the new "looey." The officer chuckled but waved his hands to quiet them down.

"Easy, listen up," he repeated. "The major wants everyone to fall in at the Eagle's Nest. We have an announcement."

"Is the war over yet?" someone hollered.

"No, not yet, sorry," said the lieutenant. He sat down and directed Roy farther up the mountain road.

Roy followed the officer's directions to a parking area fronting a massive tunnel carved into the mountain. "Park here," the lieutenant said.

Mac looked around. "This is the Eagle's Nest?"

"No, the Eagle's Nest is up there." The airborne officer pointed to the top of the mountain. "We go through this tunnel to an elevator that leads to the Nest. Follow me."

The tunnel burrowed almost four hundred feet into the mountain. Marble bricks lined its yawing maw and its shaft. Overhead, electric lamps lit the tunnel, which was tall and wide enough for a large truck to pass through, though not to turn around in. Once inside the tunnel, even a vehicle as small as a jeep would have to back out. Mac eyed the massive underground structure and, remembering the bunker in Nuremburg, muttered, "The krauts and their tunnels."

A brass elevator stood at the end of the tunnel. Faux-candle electric lights illuminated its circular waiting area, also lined in marble. The lieutenant pressed a button and turned to the team. "There's a large diesel engine—someone told me it came from a U-boat—that runs a generator to power the elevator and the Eagle's Nest. Everything in the house is electric, even the stoves."

"Is this the only way to get to the Nest?" asked Harry.

"No, there's also a road, but I thought I'd give you the nickel tour."

The lieutenant pushed the call button and the elevator doors slid open. The three OSS operators gasped at the sight of the lustrous interior of polished solid brass and circular Venetian mirrors. Leather-covered benches lined three sides of the car. Eight recessed lamps arranged in an overhead circle showered the car in bright light. The soldiers stepped in, and the door closed behind them. With a slight jerk and hum, the elevator began its ascent. After a few moments, the elevator shuddered to a halt, and the door slid open.

"Gentlemen," the lieutenant said. "Welcome to the Eagle's Nest."

Chapter 24

STEINER'S SMALL CONVOY ROLLED deeper behind the American lines. They saw few American troops and only an occasional Allied plane, which would zoom low over them and, once satisfied with their identity, fly on. The few GIs they saw simply waved and plodded on.

It was mid-morning. They had spent the night before hidden in a veil of trees just off the road. It was there they learned by radio of the Fuhrer's death. The news made Rockenhäuser question the need to continue the mission.

"But, Hans, with Hitler gone, is not the war over?" he had asked. "What need does the Fuhrer have for this … relic, this … talisman now?"

Steiner didn't answer. He stared into the dark, the muscles in his jaw tightening and loosening. Finally, he turned to Rockenhäuser. "Gather the men."

Once the SS troops fell in, Steiner addressed them.

"Men, soldiers of the Reich, our Fuhrer is dead," he said. Cries of shock, bewilderment, and disbelief came from the men. "He died heroically defending Berlin—no, more than that, defending our Fatherland and our party. He is gone, but I want you to understand this. The war is not yet over. Germany is *not* lost! The party is *not* dead. We, the

Schutzstaffel, are not finished with our chores. With or without victory, the party continues and what we seek on this mission is crucial to its continuation. So, we push on and we will continue to push on until our last dying breath. *Our honor is called loyalty!*"

In a shout, the soldiers repeated the SS motto.

It was a stirring speech, but Rockenhäuser still doubted the need to continue the mission—though only silently. It would only be a matter of days—perhaps hours—until Berlin fell to the Reds. Once that happened, the Nazi Party would be without a country. Most of the Nazified countries in Europe had been or were being conquered. Perhaps the party could find a new home in fascist Spain—Rockenhäuser was certain many party bigwigs had already fled there— or in certain pro-Nazi South American countries. But it would not be their country, their Fatherland, their Germany. What would they be serving? But then, he was a soldier of the party—he had sworn a blood oath to it—and soldiers simply followed orders. What was it Steiner had told him? *Ours is not to reason why ...*

He sighed and shrugged.

"What is it, Franz?" Steiner asked.

Rockenhäuser buried his treasonous thoughts. He gestured to the passing scenery—scattered stands of trees bordered by meadows of tall grass. "This countryside reminds

me of better times. You do remember we've been here before?"

"Of course." Steiner nodded. Much of their SS training
took place in this part of Germany. "Better times," he repeated.

A swooshing sound came from their left, and the second
truck in the convoy burst into flames with a thunderous explosion even before they spotted the smoke trail left by the
anti-tank rocket. Agonizing screams mixed with the rattle
of machine gun fire and bellowed commands. Rockenhäuser swerved the jeep to the right and bounced off the asphalt
road into a thicket, the remaining truck following close behind. The SS troops bounded from the truck and took up
defensive positions around it. Steiner and Rockenhäuser
sheltered behind the jeep.

"Scheisse!" Steiner cursed as he watched SS soldiers
tumble from the burning truck and writhe on the ground,
their uniforms afire.

"In English, Hans," Rockenhäuser chided. "You told the
men to curse in English."

"Shit!" Steiner repeated. He peeked over the jeep and
spotted the machine gun on a slight rise overlooking the
roadway. "Blösch!"

The Scharführer crawled from his position. "Sir?"

"That machine gun is on that rise to the left. See it?"

"I spotted it, yes, sir."

"Take half the men and flank it from the left," Steiner ordered. "The rest will remain here and provide covering fire."

"Yes, sir."

Blösch crawled back to his original position, tapped four men on the back, and beckoned them to follow him. Together, they dashed to the left, hunched over, and protected only by the tall grass and the covering fire of the remaining SS soldiers. They worked their way through a small clump of trees until they were well to the left of the hillock with the machine gun. One by one, they crossed the road and disappeared into another thicket of trees. When they came to the edge of the trees, they were slightly behind the machine gun nest and to its right. Without hesitating, the SS soldiers opened up on the gun emplacement with rifle fire and thrown grenades.

It was over in seconds. Blösch led his men in a dash across the field and up the rise, and stopped, not understanding what he saw. The two SS officers came running from the opposite direction. They, too, halted abruptly, staring at the three bodies.

"They're all civilians, sir," Blösch said.

"Jewish partisans?" Steiner questioned.

Resistance fighters constantly harassed German occupation troops in Europe and Russia. These included bands of Jewish partisans who had either escaped from the camps or had avoided arrest. Most of the organized Jewish partisan bands were in Russia and eastern Europe, not Germany. But in recent weeks, with the Allied noose tightening around Germany's neck, many new bands had formed, intent on wreaking revenge on the Nazis.

"Major?" An SS soldier leaned over one body. The dead man was young and had once been handsome with blond hair. Now half his face was gone, and blood and brain tissue matted his hair.

"I know this man. We trained together. He's SS."

The soldier knelt and felt around the corpse's neck until he found a thin leather lanyard. Threaded onto the strap was an oval German military identity disc. He held it up for Steiner to see.

"Werwölfen," Steiner muttered.

The soldier didn't understand. "Sir?"

"German resistance fighters," Steiner explained. "One of Colonel Skorzeny's projects. Turning the tables, so to speak, on the Allied occupiers."

"But why attack us?" Rockenhäuser asked.

Steiner pinched the collar of Rockenhäuser's GI-issued jacket. "Why do you think?"

Rockenhäuser nodded, understanding.

"Staff sergeant," Steiner said. "Bury our men." He pointed toward the stand of trees on the far side of the road.

"Over there, in the shade. And take those damn American coats and shirts off them. Bury them in their SS tunics."

"Yes, sir."

The young SS soldier still knelt next to the attacker he knew. "Major, what about them?"

Steiner looked down at the soldier, who held the dead man's identity disc up. He nodded. "Bury them, too, sergeant."

"Yes, sir." The Scharführer beckoned his men to pick up the bodies.

A corporal chugged up the hill and reported to Steiner. "What's the butcher's bill?" Steiner demanded.

"All but one in the truck are dead, sir," the corporal said. "A lucky strike in the fuel tank turned the truck into a fire ball."

"Not so lucky for our men," Rockenhäuser muttered.

Steiner ignored him. "And the survivor?"

"Badly wounded, major," the corporal said. "A fragment penetrated his abdomen. He's dying, but it is going to take some time."

Steiner nodded, grimacing. He glanced at Blösch. "Staff sergeant, you know what must be done."

"Yes, sir."

Blösch trudged back to what remained of the convoy. The wounded soldier lay on his back behind the smoldering truck, his knees up in the way the first aid instructors had taught them to treat belly wounds. A battle dressing placed over the wound was soaked through with blood. The Scharführer gazed at the wounded man. He, too, was young, hardly more than nineteen, with youthful good looks and dark hair that matched his dark eyes. The eyes looked back at Blösch, dull and unfocused. Blösch pointed his Tommy gun at the youth's head. "Sorry, son," he said, then pulled the trigger.

The ground was soft where they dug the graves. With shovels taken from the two trucks, they dug eleven graves— eight for the SS men in the truck and three for the Werwölfen who killed them. When they finished, Steiner stood over the graves and muttered some words he remembered from a burial service he once attended. He raised his arm in the Nazi salute and shouted, "Our honor is called loyalty!"

After the survivors had echoed his salute, Steiner turned and marched toward the remaining truck and jeep, Rockenhäuser on his heels.

"What should we do about the destroyed truck?"

"Leave it," Steiner said. "The Amis will think it was ambushed and its occupants captured—" He stopped mid-sentence and reconsidered. "But have Blösch go over it and make certain there is nothing on it that might betray us." He glanced at a watch on his wrist. "And be fast about it. We've lost too much time already."

Chapter 25

CORPORAL WILBERT BLUETZ DROPPED his Mauser rifle and struggled to slip out of his field kit before his intestines exploded. For the past three days and nights, Bluetz's bowels had growled and burbled and spit out what little food he had eaten. If it could be called food. Putrid horse meat torn from some poor stupid animal slaughtered in the crossfire of war. Unknown berries plucked from any bush he and his comrades happened upon. Some rancid cheese from a bombed-out farmhouse. And water from streams that, for all they knew, were littered upstream with the moldering bodies of men and animals alike.

They had been on their own for more than a week, stragglers separated from their unit in the rush to stay ahead of the Allied advance. There had been seven of them, all from the same company of infantry. One of them, poor old Willie Stuz, half crazed with thirst and hunger, staggered into a minefield and that was the end of him. Yet, his death had saved the others from entering that minefield and meeting the same end. They gave the field a wide berth, just another detour on a long, endless march of death.

Bluetz loosened his belt and trousers, dropped them, and squatted as what felt like his entire insides squirted out of him. From the distance came the murmuring of his comrades resting in the shade of roadside trees. No doubt they were discussing the same topic they had been debating for days—why go on? It was obvious the war was lost and soon to be finished. They had no idea where their company was, or even if it still existed. For that matter, they had no idea where *any* of the German army was. Why not surrender? Better to choose who you surrendered to—such as the Amis or the Tommies—than to be captured by the vengeful French who were likely to shoot a surrendering German soldier or, worse, *the Russians*. The mere thought of capture by the Russians seized his bowels with another cramp and more squirting ensued. Bluetz, like many of his comrades, had heard the stories told by the few German POWs who escaped Russian captivity. Better to face the French and die quickly than to be caught by the Reds.

His comrades' murmurings grew louder. Arguing, he thought. The first gunshot so startled him, he nearly fell backward into his own liquefied excrement. More gunfire ensued, and he hauled up his trousers and grabbed for his rifle and ammo belt. His boot slipped on the gooey mess he'd left, and he fell forward onto the ground. Lying there, bullets zipped overhead like angry insects, slicing off the tops of the grass like a scythe. With his Mauser in his left hand and his kit in the right, he scuttled toward the firing and his friends.

The firing stopped. Bluetz heard new voices, strange voices speaking stranger words. He poked his head above the grass and saw men wearing baggy green fatigues and bowl-shaped helmets moving around the bodies of his fellow soldiers. *Russians!*

Bluetz ducked and scuttled in the opposite direction. Panicked, he let the rifle and his kit slip from his hands so he could crawl faster, putting more distance between him and the barbarous Red soldiers, while his brain screamed, *Why did we not surrender to the Amis when we had a chance to?*

☼

Valery's point man came back at a trot, waving at the Spetsnaz soldiers to take cover at the side of the road. Reaching Valery's position, the soldier threw himself to the ground, gulping for air.

"Germans, Comrade Captain," he said between gasps.

"How many?"

"Not many. Maybe a half dozen." The soldier shook his head. "About half a kilometer. They are only sitting there on this side of the road. No pickets. No defensive positions."

"Probably stragglers," Valery said. He called to his serzhánt and Alexeyev moved closer. "About a half dozen German infantry, half a kilometer ahead," Valery said. "No defensive positions. I think they're probably stragglers."

"You want us to take them or kill them?"

"We have no need for prisoners," Valery said. "And we can't let them see us and warn anyone. Understood?"

"Understood, Comrade Captain."

Alexeyev selected five men and led them through the brush lining the roadside. A quarter of an hour later, they heard the Germans and a short while after that saw them lounging at the edge of the road. The scout was correct. They were in no defensive posture. Looking at them, the Russian sergeant thought the Germans felt the war was already over. Too bad for them, it wasn't.

Motioning to his men to follow him, Alexeyev rose from the grass and leveled his PPSh-41 submachine gun with a drum magazine. His men stood, aiming their Tokarev SVT-40 semi-automatic rifles. At first glance, the German stragglers thought they were seeing ghosts rise from the grassland. By the time they realized the figures were Soviet soldiers, it was too late to grab their weapons. They raised their arms and shouted, *"Russisch Kamerad! Kamerad!"*

Alexeyev glanced at his men and nodded. A single first shot was followed by a fusillade as the Russians quick-fired their SVTs. With another nod from Alexeyev, the firing stopped. Alexeyev crossed the road and fired a long *coup de grâce* burst at the bodies. Then he slung his weapon and lit a cigarette.

Valery and the rest of his men arrived minutes later. He studied the crumpled bodies, noting the rifles scattered at a distance from the corpses. "This is all of them?" he asked.

"Yes, Comrade Captain," Alexeyev said. "They didn't put up a fight."

"I can see that," Valery said. "Pull the bodies into the tall grass and conceal them. Then we will continue."

☼

Corporal Bluetz heard voices again and chanced another look. There were more Russian soldiers now. One appeared to be an officer. The Russians dragged the bodies of his comrades into the taller grass and left them. Bluetz watched the Reds march away, waiting for a full half hour to ensure there were not more behind them. When he was confidant no more Russians were coming, he rose and scurried away from the road. He didn't know where he was headed, only that he wanted to be as far away from the Russians as possible.

Chapter 26

THE ELEVATOR LEFT THEM in a small entrance hall. Opposite the lift was a hallway which the lieutenant explained led to the lavatories, a guardroom, a kitchen, and a room set aside as a study for Hitler. To the right, stairs led to a large dining room. Like the tunnel leading to the elevator, granite blocks lined the walls. GI graffiti marred the immaculate stonework with soldiers' names and the year, the ubiquitous "Killroy was here," and a few doodles that questioned the legitimacy of the birth of various well-known Nazi elites.

They took the stairs leading into the dining room, which extended to either side of the door. There, varnished wood-panel walls contrasted with the masonry they'd seen so far. A handsome lacquered wooden table stood in the middle of the dining room, surrounded by thirty chairs scattered about. Empty wine, champagne, and schnapps bottles littered the table.

"A lot of celebratory drinking, I see," said Mac.

"We discovered Hermann Goering's personal wine cellar and liberated its contents," the lieutenant said with a sheepish grin. "It was a *big* cellar."

Windows filled the far wall with an expansive view of the surrounding mountains. Beyond the window, a sun-bathed terrace offered the same view. Stairs led to an octagonal reception hall, again dressed in granite brickwork. Windows embedded in each segment of the wall provided a two-hundred-and-seventy-degree view of the Bavarian Alps. Standing against the nearest wall was a magnificent marble fireplace, part of its mantel chipped away by souvenir hunters. A great round table cluttered with empty bottles stood in the center of the room, surrounded by scattered sofas and lounge chairs. Soldiers played cards at the table while others napped on the chairs and sofas.

The lieutenant strode into the hall. "All right, Easy Company, listen up!"

Muttered moans and groans greeted him, and he repeated himself. There was more of the same until someone glanced up and recognized the officer.

"Well, well," a soldier said. "Look at the baby looey!"

The room came alive with friendly jeers and cat-calls, which the second lieutenant took in stride. He fluttered his hands to quiet down the room.

"The major wants Easy to fall in," he said when the room quieted. "These officers here want to address you all."

"You can address me and mail me back to the States," someone yelled.

Another asked, "Is the war over?"

"Not yet," said the lieutenant. "We still have a few fräuleins to conquer." This resulted in several dirty remarks before he continued. "All right, muster outside. On the double."

The paratroopers gathered in a circular turnaround at the end of the road leading up from Obersalzberg. Several paratroopers were already there, having hiked up the hill from the Berghof. The lieutenant climbed onto a jeep parked in the turnaround and endured more taunts before the crowd quieted.

"These officers are from the OSS," he began.

"Special services?" a voice cried out. "You putting on a show?"

Another shouted, "Got any dames with you? Ain't no entertainment without dames."

The lieutenant quieted the men down again. "Office of *Strategic Services*. You know, the guys who organized and fought with the resistance in France. They were fighting in France before we jumped into Normandy."

That sobered the crowd. The lieutenant jumped down and Mac and Harry took his place. Harry carried his replica of the Spear of Destiny.

"My name is MacAuley," Mac said. "Captain MacAuley. This is Lieutenant Herschel, and that's Staff Sergeant Damper. We're on orders from General Patton to—"

The soldiers interrupted Mac with raspberries and boos, and one soldier yelled, "We didn't need no rescuing from Bastogne!"

Mac smiled and waved his hands to silence the hecklers. "Understood," he said. "But Patton gets his orders from Ike. And Ike wants us to find an ancient relic that Hitler stole from a museum in Vienna—"

"A what-ic?" a voice asked.

"A relic," another answered. "Something real old."

"Show them, Harry."

Harry opened the box with the faux spear blade and held it up. "This is a replica of an ancient blade from a spear dating back to Biblical times. The Nazis stole it and we're looking for it."

"We think Hitler might have hidden it in the Berghof," Mac said. "Since Easy Company has been … souvenir hunting … in there, we thought one of you might have found it."

This time, there were no wisecracks or jeers.

"If any of you have it, you're not in trouble," Mac assured them. "You have every right to hunt for souvenirs. But ownership of this relic—this spear—has international repercussions, and Allied HQ wants to return it to its rightful owner."

More silence. The paratroopers stared balefully at the OSS officers.

Mac turned to Harry. "This is getting us nowhere," he said. "You're the master interrogator. If you spoke to each of the men, you think you could figure out if one of them has the spear?"

"Mac, this is a full infantry company," Harry said. "There's got to be more than a hundred men."

"And we've got plenty of time," Mac said. "Unless you've got a better idea?" Harry shook his head. "Okay, while you talk to them, Roy and I will retrieve our jeep and head back down to the Berghof and scour the place." Mac turned to the airborne lieutenant. "Lieutenant, have your men fall in, in proper company formation, by platoons. Send them inside to talk to Lieutenant Herschel one at a time."

"Sir?"

Mac jumped off the jeep. "You heard me, lieutenant."

"Yes, sir."

There was little left to scour in the Berghof. What bombs didn't demolish, the retreating SS burned. Anything left standing was opened, tossed over, or torn apart by soldiers seeking mementos of their capture of Hitler's vacation home. Roy found an unopened wine bottle and pried the cork out with his OSS-issued Fairbairn–Sykes fighting knife. He and Mac sat in chairs on the Berghof's patio, taking turns with the bottle and enjoying the scenery.

"That was quite the task you put Harry on, Mac," Roy said. "You really think he'll turn up something?"

Mac shook his head. "No, but I didn't have any other ideas." He handed the bottle to Roy.

Roy took a swig. "He might," he said. "Harry's a bright boy."

"Maybe he will," agreed Mac. He took the bottle back and drank.

They had nearly emptied the bottle when a jeep approached. The vehicle, driven by the paratroop officer, pulled up alongside their jeep and Harry jumped out with another soldier in tow.

Mac and Roy stared at the two and Roy muttered, "My God, Harry did it."

"Mac, meet Private Bourne," Harry said. "He had a guilty conscience and came to me saying he might have the spear."

MacAuley looked at the soldier. "Might?"

"Well, I think it is," Bourne said. "It's in a box like the lieutenant's spear is in, but I didn't look at it too good before I hid it."

"Why did you hide it?" Mac asked.

The soldier looked uneasy. He glanced at the paratroop lieutenant, who simply nodded.

"I hid it from Lieutenant Snyder," he said. "He's been taking all the good loot—I mean, souvenirs. Before I found this spear thing, I found an album full of pictures of Hitler and other Nazi krauts. Snyder saw it and took it. Said he was confiscating it. But he wasn't confiscating it. He took it to add to the rest of his loot."

Mac looked at the airborne officer who said, "Lieutenant Snyder is our battalion supply officer and a ... *scavenger* of great repute."

Mac considered the situation, then glanced at the private. "Photo album, you said?"

"Yes, sir," Bourne said.

"You stay here with Lieutenant Herschel," Mac said. He started walking toward their jeep. "Roy, you're with me."

☼

They looked for Snyder at battalion headquarters, but a supply sergeant said the lieutenant had not been in all day. He suggested they look for him at the gasthaus, a small local hotel commandeered to billet officers. They found him with his own private suite of rooms filled with the spoils of his endeavors.

"Quite a collection you have here, Lieutenant Snyder," Mac said as they entered the suite without knocking.

Snyder was lying in bed, still in skivvies, smoking a cigar and drinking tea out of a silver tea service. "Who the hell are you?" he demanded.

"That's 'who the hell are you, *captain*'," Mac said. "MacAuley. Intelligence. We're here to examine your collection for anything that might provide some intelligence value."

Mac and Roy split up, each taking a side of the room, and began rummaging through Snyder's collection.

"Intelligence?" Snyder said, struggling to pull on his trousers. "What for? The war is over."

"Is it? I haven't heard that yet," Mac said. "Have you, sergeant?"

"Negative, sir," Roy said. He picked up a file folder and opened it. "Holy—!"

Roy handed the folder over to Mac. It contained hundreds of pornographic photos. He closed it and tossed it on the bed. "I don't see any intelligence value in those, do you, sergeant?"

"No, sir," Roy said. "Unless the medical service needs some intelligence on Nazi gynecology."

Mac spotted what looked like a leather-bound album and opened it. Inside were photographs of Hitler, his dog, his mistress Eva Braun, and a rogue's gallery of Nazi officials. "Now this, however, does have intelligence value."

Mac handed it to Roy, who flipped through the pages, nodding. "I'll say …"

"It's just photos of Hitler and a bunch of Nazis," Snyder said. "What intelligence value is that?"

Mac turned and stepped threateningly toward Snyder, who backed away. "After the war, there will be war-crime trials," he said. "Those photos can help identify who will stand trial. You had this in your possession and didn't bring it to your superiors? That's withholding evidence, lieutenant. You're in big trouble. Big trouble." Mac glanced around the room. "Your battalion commander will hear about this." He waved a hand around the room. "About all of this."

He turned and marched out the door, Roy right behind him. Driving off in the jeep, they both laughed.

"You played that a little over the top, didn't you, Mac?" Roy said.

"Couldn't help it," Mac said. "I've been playing Nazi officers for too long."

Chapter 27

MAC AND ROY RETURNED to the Berghof where Harry, Bourne, and their airborne lieutenant escort were waiting. Mac handed Bourne the confiscated photo album. "A fair trade," Mac told him. "The photo album for what you *think* may be the spear. Deal?"

Bourne's eyes grew large as he looked at the book in MacAuley's hand. "Deal, sir. Yes, sir!"

"Good, now where is the spear?"

"The battalion has us billeted in what's left of the SS barracks over there, sir." Bourne pointed to the Alpine-style barracks his major had mentioned to Mac earlier. "I hid it in there."

"Lead the way," Mac said.

The young private led them across a crater-strewn field toward a cluster of modern buildings built to house and feed the hundreds of SS soldiers who guarded Hitler's residence and its environs. The complex had not escaped the fury of the British bombing, and several of the buildings were collapsed or heavily damaged.

"This barracks complex has all the comforts of home," the airborne officer said. "Besides the barracks, there's a gymnasium, mess hall, motor pool garage, parade ground, even a shooting range." He pointed to a house-like structure to the left. "That was HQ for the SS."

"How much is still habitable?" Harry asked.

"Most of it," the lieutenant said. "The RAF did a job on this place, but the bombing wasn't as complete as they hoped."

"Better than sleeping in a foxhole," Bourne added.

The private led them into the barracks and up a flight of stairs. "Wait here, sirs," Bourne said. "Nothing personal, but I don't want anyone to know my hiding place. If word got back to Lieutenant Snyder …"

"Understood, soldier," Mac said. "Carry on."

Bourne disappeared into a room. When he appeared several minutes later, he carried a rectangular box, but not the photo album. "Here it is, sir," he said, handing the box to Mac. "Is this what you're looking for?"

Mac opened the box and peered inside. Nodding, he said, "I think it is, private. Thank you."

"Thank *you*, sir," Bourne said. "I got my photo album back."

"If you don't mind telling," Harry asked, "how'd you find the spear and where?"

"In the damaged part of the Berghof where a bomb hit, there's a collapsed wall," Bourne said. "I was looking for loot—souvenirs after Lieutenant Snyder took my album. Under the debris, I found this wall safe. It looked like the bomb blast broke it open. The box with that spear thing was inside."

They returned to the jeeps, and Bourne and his lieutenant drove back up the hill to the Eagle's Nest. Mac handed the box to Harry, who opened it and showed it to Roy. Inside was an identical blade to Harry's replica.

"Well?" Mac said.

"I'll be right back," Harry said, disappearing inside the ruined Berghof. A few minutes later, he returned, the box in one hand and the spear held in the other. "It's a fake," he said, shaking his head.

☼

"I don't understand," Roy said. "Why would Hitler keep a fake spear in a wall safe?"

Harry opened the footlocker bolted to the jeep and placed his replica and Hitler's inside. "I don't think he knew it was fake."

"That doesn't make sense," Roy protested. "The infallible Der Führer not knowing something?"

Two GIs walked out of the woods leading three German soldiers in dirty and tattered SS field uniforms. As they approached the jeep, the one wearing corporal stripes yelled out, "Hey, Joe, can you spare a smoke?" As Mac and Harry turned, the GI spotted the silver bars on each man's collar. "Oh, sorry, sirs. Didn't realize you were officers."

"No problem, soldier," Mac said. He took a fresh pack of cigarettes from the footlocker and tossed it to the soldier. "Keep it."

"Hey, thanks, captain," the corporal said, ripping open the pack. "I gave these guys my last butts." He nodded to the POWs. "They looked like they needed them more than me."

"Where'd you find them?" Mac asked.

"Up the mountain in the woods," the other soldier, a private, said.

"Battalion has us running patrols looking for stragglers or those partisans they call werewolves," said the corporal. "From the little German I know, I understand they'd been out there hiding since the limeys bombed this place."

While Roy chatted with the GIs, Mac took three K-ration packages from the locker and offered them to the SS soldiers. "*Verpflegung.*"

The empty, sunken eyes of the Germans grew large at the sight of the offered rations. Hesitant at first, their hunger overrode any sense of caution or mistrust, and they stepped forward and snatched the packages and tore them open, repeating, "*Danke. Danke.*"

Mac took another pack of smokes from the locker and handed them to a prisoner. "*Teilen*" Share.

The POW ripped open the pack, took one out, and passed cigarettes to his comrades. They each found a pack of matches in the K-rations and lit their cigarettes. The prisoner smiled at his captors, then glanced into the footlocker. He pointed at the replica lance blades and said, "Der Speer!"

Harry spoke to the soldier in German. "You know what that is?"

"Yes!" the POW answered. "The Spear of Destiny. But those cannot be real."

"Why do you say that?" Harry asked.

Despite his tattered uniform, the prisoner seemed to puff up with pride. "I once had the honor of guarding the real spear and the other Holy Relics when the reichsführer came to see them," he answered.

"When was that?" Harry asked.

"In Vienna, after the Anschluss," the POW said. "Before Der Führer arrived."

Harry glanced at Mac, who nodded back.

"Himmler saw the spear *before* Hitler?" Harry asked.

"Ja."

"What did he do when he saw it?"

The German shrugged. "He ordered me to go outside and smoke," he said. "I did not go back in until he came out."

"Did Himmler have access to the relics?"

The German nodded. "He took my keys that opened the display case."

"When he came in, was he carrying anything?"

The prisoner nodded again. "A briefcase, as he always did."

Harry looked at Mac again, who urged him on with another nod.

"When Himmler left, did you notice anything different about the display?"

"*Nein.*" The German paused, his eyes focused on a distant memory. "Wait. I did notice two small drops of blood, one inside the case and one outside. I assumed the reichsführer cut himself while examining the spear. I cleaned them up with a handkerchief before Der Führer arrived."

The corporal stepped up. "Sorry, sirs," he said, "but we should be getting these krauts down to battalion S-2."

"Sure, corporal, go ahead," Mac said, reverting to English.

"Thanks for the smokes, sir," the corporal said as he began prodding the prisoners. The Germans, clutching their rations, reluctantly moved on.

"What was all that kraut talk about?" Roy asked as the prisoners and their captors left.

"Himmler has the real spear," Mac said.

"It makes sense," Harry said. "Hitler used the occult for propaganda purposes, but Himmler was the true believer. He sent SS units all over the world looking for mythological items he believed would bring greater power to the Reich."

"More likely himself," Mac said.

"That, too," Harry conceded. "Himmler has always considered himself the true power behind the Nazi throne. And he actually believes in the Spear of Destiny legend. Remember I told you Himmler had a replica of the spear that he kept in his office? He must have used that one to replace the True Spear even before Hitler arrived to view the Holy Relics."

"Later, when we started bombing Nuremburg, Himmler must have ordered the most valuable relics removed from the bunker in Nuremberg for further safe keeping," Mac said. "But he left behind the spear because he knew it was fake."

"Because *he* had the True Spear," Harry added.

"I ask my question again," said Roy. "Why would Hitler keep a fake spear in a wall safe in his personal residence?"

"Because he didn't *know* it was fake," Harry said. "Before the Anschluss, Himmler publicly presented Hitler a replica spear, promising he would soon have the real one. Hitler had to believe the one on display in Nuremberg was the True Spear and—even not being a true believer himself—he wanted it. Hitler considered himself the new messiah, and the new messiah had to own the Spear of Destiny, even if its powers were only mythical."

Mac added, "At some point, he replaced the Nuremberg spear with his replica—"

"Only Hitler didn't know the one on display was also fake," concluded Roy. "Okay, I gotcha."

"And that means Himmler has the real thing," added Mac.

"So, where does that leave us?" Roy asked. "If Himmler kept the real spear in his office in Berlin, the Russians will find it before we can get there."

Harry shook his head. "Not in Berlin," he said. "Just like Hitler wanted to keep what he thought was the real spear in a place that was special to him, Himmler would want to keep the real spear someplace special to *him*."

"And that would be …? Mac asked.

"Wewelsburg Castle," Harry replied. "The holiest of holy places for the SS."

Chapter 28

CORPORAL WILBERT BLUETZ STAGGERED along the side of a road. His diarrhea and lack of water left him dehydrated, yet his bowels still rumbled. Every few minutes, a fresh wave of cramps sent him scampering into the nearby trees where he squirted out the last few drops of whatever bodily fluids he still retained. As he walked, his dry, caked lips moved in silent muttering. *Where am I? Where is everyone else? Has the war ended, and everyone went home?* He chuckled at the thought. *My luck. The war ends and no one tells me.*

But the war wasn't over. There was still the crump of artillery fire in the distance. *But here ... here I hear birds singing and bugs buzzing. Perhaps I should just sit down here and let the war come to me.*

Another cramp seized him. He slipped off the road into a stand of trees to relieve himself. As Bluetz pulled up his trousers, he heard another sound. Engines. Vehicles on the road and, by their increasing growl, Bluetz realized they were drawing near. Remembering the ambush of his comrades by Russian troops, he stayed hidden behind a tree, waiting for the vehicles to appear.

He spotted them a few minutes later. A jeep with two passengers and a large truck with several soldiers. Both bore white stars. *His heart jumped. Amis! American soldiers!*

Bluetz slipped from behind the tree and, with his arms raised, walked toward the road yelling, "Kamerad! Nicht schießen!" *Comrade! Do not shoot!*

The vehicles slowed to a stop, and the man in the jeep's passenger seat raised an American carbine in Bluetz's direction. The soldiers in the truck raised their rifles as well. Well, that was to be expected, Bluetz thought. The war isn't over. They had to be careful.

Bluetz set a big, painful smile on his desiccated lips and continued walking forward, shouting, "Kamerad! Nicht schießen!" Next, he tried the English phrase he had been secretly practicing for weeks. "I sur … ren … der!"

The soldier with the carbine, obviously an officer, stepped out of the jeep and beckoned Bluetz toward him. "Kommen sie hier!" *Come here!*

Wonderful! The Ami officer speaks some German, Bluetz thought. That'll make it easier to talk with him.

As Bluetz reached the road, the officer opened his jacket. Underneath the American uniform, Bluetz recognized the gray battle dress and insignia of the Waffen SS. Bluetz's smile faded as his steps faltered.

"Kommen sie hier!" the officer repeated.

Bluetz forced the smile back onto his face, lowered his arms, and stepped toward the officer. "Mein Herr!" he exclaimed, saluting. He added in German, "I am saved!"

"What is your name?" the officer demanded, also in German.

"Corporal Wilbert Bluetz," Bluetz answered.

"Where is your unit?"

Bluetz shook his head. "I don't know. My comrades and I were separated from it in the retreat. We were trying to make it back to our lines."

"Your comrades?" the officer said. He glanced toward the cluster of trees Bluetz emerged from. "There are more of you? Where are they?"

"No, no, mein Herr," Bluetz said, shaking his head again. "Dead. Ambushed by Russian soldiers." He pointed back the way he came. "On the far side of those trees. Three, maybe four kilometers."

"Russian soldiers? This far west? Impossible."

"But they are, mein Herr," Bluetz said. "I saw them myself. They were speaking Russian."

"You *saw* them and *heard* them?" the officer repeated. "Where were you when your comrades were killed?"

Bluetz placed both hands on his stomach. "I am not well, mein Herr. I have the shits—something I ate. I was relieving myself in the brush when the Russians appeared."

The troops in the truck snickered. The officer said, "Yes, I can smell it on you. Where is your weapon?"

"I lost it in the brush," Bluetz said. "I dropped it trying to evade the Russians."

"You didn't use it to kill the Russians before they killed your comrades?"

"It happened so fast," Bluetz said. "They were all dead by the time I got my pants back up."

More snickers from the truck.

"So, you abandoned your fellow soldiers, and then you surrender to the first Amis you think you see." The officer pulled a handkerchief from his pocket and wiped sweat from his eyes. "That's what you're telling me?"

"Ye-yes—well, no, mein Herr," Bluetz stammered. "It wasn't like that."

"You are a disgrace to your uniform, to the army, to Germany, and to the party," the officer said. "Scharführer, you know what we do with deserters."

"Yes, Herr Sturmbannführer!" A staff sergeant stepped from the cab of the truck and pointed to two soldiers in the rear bed. The soldiers jumped down and followed the noncom as he grabbed Bluetz by the shoulder and pushed him off the road. Bluetz tried to protest, but the sergeant slugged him in the stomach and dragged him farther off the road. The stomach blow caused Bluetz's bowels to cramp, and he fouled himself.

"Stand up like a soldier," the sergeant yelled.

Bluetz straightened the best he could. Tears streamed from his eyes, weaving little rivulets along his grimy face. As if in a nightmare, he watched the two SS soldiers fall in before him and raise their rifles. The sergeant stood to the side, his eyes on the officer, who eyed Bluetz for a moment before letting the handkerchief slip from his hand.

☼

The rifle shots sounded unusually loud in the otherwise quiet woods. Scharführer Blösch dismissed the two soldiers, and the three hustled back to the truck. Steiner picked up his handkerchief, slipped it back into his pocket, and took his seat in the jeep.

"The old handkerchief signal again, eh, Hans?" Rockenhäuser said.

Steiner pulled a map from the jeep's glove compartment and unfolded it on his lap.

"If and when this war ever ends," he said, "I want no one able to testify that I gave a verbal order to execute any-one."

"But Blösch understands what the handkerchief means," Rockenhäuser said.

"Blösch is not a worry," Steiner said. "And if he ever becomes one, he'll be taken care of."

"And the men, Hans?" Rockenhäuser asked.

Steiner turned to his second in command. "I have never ordered you to shoot anyone, have I, Franz?"

"No," Rockenhäuser said. "No, you haven't."

Steiner glanced at his wristwatch, folded the map, and replaced it in the glove compartment. "Let us go, then," he said. "We lost too many hours detouring around that blown bridge this morning, and we still have a ways to go."

Chapter 29

ROY USED A SIPHON TO *liberate* gasoline from the Nazi staff cars left abandoned, refilling the jeep's tank and the jerry can tied to its hood. He also filled two more gas cans liberated from a bomb-damaged Kübelwagen and lashed them to the sides of the jeep. It was over four hundred miles to Wewelsburg in northern Germany, and they would need the extra gas.

They took turns driving the ten hours to Wewelsburg. Roy also liberated a siren from one of the staff cars, wired it into the jeep's electrical system, and used it to clear the Autobahn ahead of them. By the time they entered Wewelsburg late in the afternoon, all their ears were ringing.

Harry pointed to a massive brick structure with three tall turrets looming over the hamlet.

"Wewelsburg Castle," he said.

"Why do you call it—what was it you said? 'The holiest of holy sites for the SS'?" Roy asked.

"Himmler took it over in the mid-thirties," Harry explained. "From what I remember reading in the German press before the war, it was originally going to be a school for the SS—a kind of Nazi West Point. But being an occultist, Himmler started turning it into a holy site for SS officers. Some of Himmler's critics refer to it as his Valhalla. Others derided it as Himmler's Grail."

"Why Grail?" Mac asked.

"Apparently, Hitler wasn't the only Nazi infatuated with the story of Sir Percival and the knights of the Round Table. Himmler designed the castle as a sort of Germanic Camelot, complete with a round table for his twelve knights."

"Knights?" Roy asked.

"That's how Himmler sees himself and his senior SS leaders," Harry said. "Knights of the SS."

"Jesus, we're looking for the Spear of Destiny in a Nazi Camelot?" Mac muttered.

"That's about it," Harry said. "Himmler spent as much time there as he could. To him, it's a holy place."

The closer they got to the castle, the more dreadful it loomed. Built in the shape of a triangle, it had three high walls, each three stories tall and topped by a peaked roof. Two tall, round, and narrow turrets with domed cupolas anchored the east and west corners, each with four stories. A broader rounded tower with a crenellated battlement anchored the north corner. A deep, dry moat surrounded the castle, backed by a thick stand of trees. Licks of black soot rose above many of the castle's windows, evidence of a fire and shattered bricks around the base of the two thinner towers revealed a failed attempt to topple them with explosives.

"Third Armored overran this area last month," Mac said. "They must've torched the castle."

"Maybe," Harry said. "Or the SS tried to destroy the castle to keep it out of Allied hands."

"Well, it doesn't look like it's in anyone's hands right now," Mac said. "The place looks deserted."

"Looks fucking haunted to me," murmured Roy.

Roy steered the jeep past a deserted brick sentry post across a masonry bridge spanning the dry moat up to the arched castle entrance standing between the two narrow towers. Mac told him to stop.

"Let's go in on foot—carefully," Mac said.

Roy parked and all three men got out with their grease guns, scanned the area, then cautiously approached the entrance, splitting apart for tactical distance. Mac entered first while Harry and Roy covered him. From the entrance, the brick courtyard narrowed until it reached the third tower. A single arched doorway led into the turret. Its charred wooden door hung from one hinge. The courtyard was empty except for scorched splinters and other burnt debris tossed about by fire-driven winds. Black soot marred both the high walls and the three towers, and the air was heavy with the lingering miasma of fiery destruction.

Mac waved the others in. They separated, each taking a side of the castle to search. A few minutes later, they met in the courtyard again.

"You have any idea where Himmler's office would be?" Mac asked.

"None," Harry replied.

"Then we search," Mac said. "Roy, go back and stay with the jeep and keep an eye out."

"Fine with me, Mac." Roy shivered and slung his grease gun. "This place gives me the creeps. You're likely to run into Boris Karloff or Bela Lugosi."

"I think what happened here would make Karloff and Lugosi both blanch," Harry said.

They entered the north tower. A breeze wafting through blown-out windows had cleared it of smoke, but not the reek of charred wood and blackened brick. Steps led down to a circular room below ground level. The only light came from small windows placed high in the walls and angled upward to catch the sun. Taking up most of the floor was a strange sunken circle, with what looked like a fire pit in the center. Around that were twelve short pedestals, over which hung twelve light sconces, now dark. A stylized swastika decorated the ceiling over the pit.

"Roy's right. This place looks haunted," Mac said. He pointed to the sunken circle. "What the hell is that?"

"Looks like some kind of eternal flame set up," Harry said. "I think this is a mausoleum or crypt."

They climbed a winding staircase to the next level and entered another massive, round room. Strange runes covered the walls, and an intricate, inlaid depiction of a sunburst decorated the floor. But instead of being brightly colored, the sun was the darkest of blacks.

"What's that supposed to be?" Mac asked.

Harry shrugged. "A black sun. An occult symbol of some sort, I guess." He waved his hand toward the rune wall hangings. "All of these are pagan symbols."

He turned a full circle, studying the room, its walls and its ceiling. In the center of the ceiling, now darkened by smoke and soot, was another oversized swastika. He counted twelve ornate columns, each joined to the others by archways. Behind the columns and arches stood tall, narrow windows overlooking Wewelsburg, their remaining glass stained with soot. Over the entrance, also barely visible through the fire damage, was an inscription.

"It says here, this is the Hall of the Generals," he said. "There are twelve columns representing each of the SS departments. I think this may be Himmler's round table where his SS generals—that is, his *knights*—met."

"Knights, my ass," muttered Mac. "A bunch of Teutonic twits. Where do we go now?"

Harry walked around the room, checking doors leading to other rooms. "The first two floors seem to be ceremonial," he said. "Administrative offices are probably upstairs, with offices of the most important officials on the highest floor."

"Makes sense," Mac said. "Crap flows downhill. Let's go."

They climbed the staircase to the upper floors, stopping at each landing to glance down the hallways leading to the smaller east and west towers. Reaching the fourth floor, they noticed a distinct difference in the architecture. The floor was more open than the others, with fewer offices, and the few offices it had were much larger, more luxurious, and arranged to focus the visitor's attention on the largest office in the west tower.

"That must be Himmler's office," Harry said.

The door was locked and bolted and, though scorched, still too thick to break down. Mac motioned Harry to stand back, and he emptied a magazine from his grease gun into the lock. The bullets splintered the door. A good shove and it swung open.

Footsteps pounded in the courtyard. Mac poked his head out of a window and saw Roy dash into the castle, weapon ready. "It's okay. We're just breaking and entering." As Roy walked back to the jeep muttering profanities, Mac and Harry entered Himmler's office.

Flames had not reached this room. A large mahogany desk, still highly polished, held pride of place, backed by two crossed Nazi flags framing a photo of Adolf Hitler. Photographs of Hitler and Himmler stood undisturbed on bookshelves. A desk frame held a picture of Himmler, his wife, and their children. Centered on the desk, enshrined in a wood-framed glass display case, was the Longinus spear.

Harry stepped to the desk, reaching for the spear. Mac grabbed him before he touched the case.

"It might be booby-trapped," Mac said. He approached the desk warily, eyeing it up and down, looking for wires, levers, pressure plates, or anything else that would indicate a booby trap. Stooping, he carefully checked the case and gently lifted it with two fingers. Satisfied, he picked up the display case and tossed it to Harry.

"Do your magic," he said.

Harry nodded and slipped out of the office. When he returned, he tossed the spear back to Mac.

"Fake," he said.

Chapter 30

CAPTAIN VALERY STOOD ON a hillock and took a map from his tunic, turning it until its landmarks matched those he saw through his binoculars. He and his men were just outside the hamlet of Wewelsburg. With his field glasses, he spotted the upper part of the castle and its three towers, two topped by domed cupolas. He assumed the soot licks above the towers' empty windows meant the castle had experienced a fire. Would that mean the spear they sought was destroyed? Perhaps. But it didn't matter to his mission. They would still need to march into the town and search the castle.

Valery heard someone hail him, and he turned to look down the hill where Serzhánt Alexeyev was beckoning him. The man he had sent to scout the village was standing next to the sergeant. Valery replaced the map in his tunic and side-stepped down the slope through soft earth and slick fallen leaves.

"Report," the captain said.

"The town is sparsely inhabited, Comrade Captain," the scout said. He squatted, brushed leaves out of his way, and started to draw in the dirt with his finger. "Most of the people are centered to the north—here. These areas surrounding the castle are vacant. There are signs posted in these areas. I do not speak or read German, but I had the sense they warned people to stay away."

The captain squatted next to the soldier and took out his map. Laying it on the ground, he pointed to areas around the castle that corresponded to the scout's drawings. "So, here, here, and here, correct?"

"That is correct," the scout said.

"What about the Americans?" Valery asked. "Are they occupying the town?"

The scout shook his head. "It appears not," he said. "I only saw one American jeep with three soldiers enter the town. I could not see where they went. The noise from the jeep faded, and that was it."

"Probably passing through," Alexeyev said. "Catching up with their advance forces to the east."

"That was my thought, too, serzhánt," the scout replied.

"Possibly," Valery said. *And possibly it is the Americans sent to find the spear,* he thought. "So, if we enter Wewelsburg from the south, we should avoid being spotted by any inhabitants?"

"Yes, Comrade Captain."

Valery took a deep breath and let it slowly slide out while he thought. He had to assume the three Americans were there for the same reason he was. But why only three? Of course, the Americans control this area, but only three soldiers to retrieve the spear when the Stavka in Moscow sent an entire platoon? Valery shook his head. It made no sense. Alexeyev was probably correct; they were just passing through on their way to the American lines. But if they were there for the spear, and they got to the castle first, what was he to do? Kill them? They were allies, at least for the time being. Well, he would have to work on that. As for now …

"Serzhánt," he said, pointing to the map. "Here is what we are going to do."

☼

Steiner brought his two-vehicle convoy to a stop and pulled out his map. They were only a few miles from Wewelsburg. He was eager to get there, recover the damn spear, and head back to their own lines. But they had been driving hard, and his men needed a break to stretch their legs and relieve themselves. He ordered Blösch to have the men fall out and take care of their needs.

"We probably should refill our petrol, Hans," Rockenhäuser said, squinting at the jeep's fuel gauge. "We've got less than a quarter of a tank left."

"Yes, yes," Steiner responded irritably. "Make it so."

Rockenhäuser climbed out of the jeep and gave the order. Soldiers removed fuel cans from the sides of the vehicles and poured their contents into the gas tanks.

"I hope we can find some more petrol in Wewelsburg," Rockenhäuser said. "If not, we may have to walk back to our lines."

"We'll find it," Steiner said dismissively.

"I hope we *don't* find any Amis there," Rockenhäuser added. He stepped away from the jeep, unbuttoned his trousers, and took a piss.

That was exactly what had Steiner so concerned. He had no intelligence from Berlin on whether the Americans had occupied Wewelsburg or moved on. It was one thing to drive through the countryside behind American lines wearing their disguises and fooling inquisitive Allied pilots. It was quite another to enter an occupied town where there could be roadblocks and guards and demands to show orders. But Wewelsburg was of no military value. It was not a crossroads or a railhead, nothing that would help with logistics or troop movements. The only thing of military import was the castle, and that had been abandoned and burnt. Steiner was certain there was no way the Amis could know about the Spear of Destiny. And, even if they did, of what military value was it to them? Hitler may have believed in its ridiculous legend, but the Americans?

Steiner had spent much of his childhood in the United States, the son of German immigrants who looked to escape the collapse of the German economy after the last war, then returned to the Fatherland when Hitler came to power. The

Americans he knew growing up were not into the occult; in fact, their Protestant background would revile the subject. He had had childhood friends whose parents would not let them go to the theater in 1931 to see Boris Karloff play a monster in the movie *Frankenstein*. No, the Americans would not send soldiers to recover or guard a myth. They were too practical. Unless …

Steiner had read a profile the Abwehr, German military intelligence, had produced on George Patton. Many feared Patton as a general. But Patton's reported beliefs in reincarnation amused Steiner. Patton believed he had lived several past lives, all of them as a soldier in long-forgotten wars. Would he be so foolish?

Perhaps so. Steiner recalled from the report how, during the battle for Normandy, Patton's army came within several miles of a German POW camp in which his own son-in-law was imprisoned. Without permission, Patton organized a task force with the sole purpose of rescuing his daughter's husband. The attack was an unmitigated failure for the Americans. Not only was the task force all but wiped out, Patton's son-in-law was gravely wounded and nearly died.

Yes, Steiner concluded, if Patton somehow knew about the spear's location, he would indeed risk recovering it. And that just added to Steiner's concerns.

Chapter 31

WHEN MAC AND HARRY returned to the jeep, they found Roy trying to communicate with a scruffy old man. Roy made wild gestures with his hands and arms, and the old man simply shrugged and replied softly in German. The man was short and thin, too thin to be healthy. He wore a baggy shirt and trousers that had once been white with black vertical stripes; the white was now a greasy shade of yellow and the black stripes had turned to gray. A purple triangular patch sat over the left breast. A black beret-like cap topped his shaven head. Pale skin hung loosely from the bones of his face, and his sunken eyes were dark and empty.

"Who's your friend?" Mac asked as he placed Himmler's fake spear into the footlocker.

"Hell if I know," Roy said. "I told him I don't *sprechen sie Deutsch*. He doesn't speak English and his French is as bad as my German. He keeps pointing to those trees, saying something about concentrated lager. *Lager*. That's a beer, right? The old boy wants a brew?"

"That would be *lagerbeir*," Harry said.

"Nein, nein," said the old man. "Ich komme aus einem Konzentrationslager."

The faces of both officers went pale. Roy saw it and asked, "What?"

"He says he's from a concentration camp," Mac said.

Roy stared at the prisoner, suddenly understanding what he was saying. The old man stared back with empty eyes.

"Who are you?" Harry asked in German. "Where is this concentration camp?"

"My name is Ludwig Jacobin," the old man said. "I am—I was a prisoner in the Niederhagen camp where the Nazis housed laborers who worked in the castle. Over there." He pointed toward the trees.

"You're Jewish?" Harry asked.

Jacobin shook his head and pointed to the purple triangle. "I am a Bible Student."

"Jehovah Witness?" Jacobin nodded. "Why are you in a concentration camp?"

"Our beliefs prevent us from recognizing Hitler's authority or take part in his war," Jacobin explained. "For that, we are imprisoned. We were brought here to work on the castle, to make the modifications Herr Himmler wanted. I am an architect by training and designed and built many structures before the Nazis came to power, so I was put in charge of organizing the work details."

"You said you *were* a prisoner," Mac said.

"We were liberated when your soldiers came through here," Jacobin said. "They gave us food and water, but now they are gone. We have to search for food, beg for it from the people of Wewelsburg. I heard your vehicle and came here hoping …" The old man shrugged.

"Roy, get on the radio and tell someone we need food and medical supplies for—" Mac turned to the old man and asked in German, "How many of you are there?"

"We were three thousand," Jacobin said. "We are now only fifty."

Mac looked at the prisoner, shocked. Slowly, he turned to Roy and said, "For fifty former concentration camp prisoners. The camp's just outside Wewelsburg, to the north."

Harry asked Jacobin, "How many died?"

"Oh, about a thousand," the old man said. "Not counting the prisoners brought in from other camps to be executed. One, maybe two years ago, work on the castle stopped and most of the prisoners went to other camps. They left us to finish a few repairs and perform maintenance."

Mac turned back to Jacobin. "We radioed to get you help," he said. "There will be a medical unit with food, water, and doctors. Until then …"

He opened the footlocker and took out several cartons of K-rations. Jacobin's dull eyes widened with disbelief as Mac handed them to him.

"Thank you. Thank you," he said, bowing in gratitude.

"The aid that's coming should reach you sometime tomorrow," Mac said. "You'll have to make do with that until then, I'm afraid."

"This is very kind. Thank you." Jacobin bowed again. As he did, he spotted Himmler's spear in the footlocker. "I see you have the reichsführer's Longinus spear."

"It's not real," Harry said. "It's just a replica."

"Of course," the old man said. "He would not keep the real one on his desk."

Mac's eyes narrowed. "What do you mean by 'the real one'?"

"The reichsführer kept the real lance in the safe," Jacobin said.

Mac and Harry glanced at each, each with the same thought. "What safe?" they blurted simultaneously.

"In the cellar of the west tower," the old man said, pointing to the narrow tower directly behind them. "The reichsführer ordered me to procure it specifically to keep the spear in."

"What's going on, guys?" Roy asked, looking from Mac to Harry to Jacobin.

"The spear is in a safe in the basement of that tower," Harry said.

The news didn't faze Roy. He simply asked, "How big a safe?"

"How big a safe?" Harry asked Jacobin.

Jacobin closed his eyes and rubbed his temple with his index finger. "Ten feet tall, the same wide, and four feet deep," he said, opening his eyes. "It was very hard to get down into the cellar. We had to remove some of the floor, lower it down, then repair the floor."

Mac turned to Damper. "Roy?"

Roy held up his bag of plastic explosives. "Not a problem, Mac."

The old man told them how and where to enter the cellar, offered his thanks again for the rations, then left them, walking back down the brickwork drive with a slow, shuffling gait.

☼

"Well?"

Roy didn't answer Mac. Instead, he walked around the safe, eyeing each inch of the behemoth. There were two combination dials, meaning two separate locking mechanisms and two separate combinations. An outer steel locking bar also secured the door. Roy nibbled his lower lip, then nodded.

"Piece of cake," he said.

"You sure, Roy?" Harry hammered the safe with his fist. "It seems awfully big and sturdy."

"No safe is unbreakable," Roy said, "if you have time and the proper tools. This brute is big but old. Guess the SS didn't have the money for a newer model." He pointed to

225

two large hinges on the left side of the door. "See how the hinges are on the *outside* of the safe? That's old school. They don't make them like this anymore because it's a vulnerability."

"You can blow the hinges off," Mac said, catching on.

"That and a little more," Roy said. "Some C4 on the hinges, that retaining bar, and along the seams of the door should open it." He looked up at the ceiling. "I'm more concerned that the ceiling might cave in."

Mac studied the ceiling and the walls. "I don't think so," he said. "Someone tried to blow up these towers and didn't succeed."

"Maybe they didn't know what they were doing," Roy said.

"Do you know what you're doing?" Mac asked. Roy nodded. "Then don't worry about it."

"I'd feel better if we had something to dampen the blast."

"Like what?" Mac asked.

"A few mattresses would help dampen the outward blast," Roy said.

"We saw some sleeping quarters in the west hall," Harry said.

Roy stooped and opened his explosives bag. "Get 'em."

While Mac and Harry hunted down bedding, Roy shaped his C4 into charges and placed them as he described.

By the time Mac and Harry came back with the mattresses, he had installed the detonation caps and was attaching them to an electric detonator. They stood the mattresses up around the safe while Roy tied them in place with electrical wire.

"That's it," Roy finally said.

He picked up the electric detonator—a small crank generator with a T-handle on top—and, trailing electrical wire behind, led them out of the cellar and up the stairs leading to the first floor. "Okay, fire in the hole," Roy said as he twisted the T-handle.

The blast shook the castle as thunder echoed through the courtyard. Dust bellowed from the cellar door. They raced back into the basement. The safe still stood where it had been, but its door lay sprawled before it. Ragged pieces of mattresses, some smoldering, littered the cellar floor.

Roy grinned at Mac. "Like I said, piece of cake."

The three of them approached the safe with the anticipation of children approaching a Christmas tree surrounded by presents and peered inside. There was only one item in the safe—a wooden framed glass display case like the one found on Himmler's desk. Inside, behind glass cracked by the explosion, lay the blade of a Roman Legionnaire's spear.

Harry removed the box, opened one end of it, and slipped the blade out. With a glance toward the others, he stepped away and, turning his back, examined the spear. Finished with his examination, he turned, holding the blade reverently with both hands, the barest smile on his lips. He nodded.

"It's the true Spear of Destiny," he said.

Mac and Roy crowded around Harry, staring down at the blade the Roman Centurion Longinus used to pierce the side of Christ. Each was speechless, mesmerized by the sight of the True Spear. No one noticed when a Russian officer entered the cellar.

"Bloody good job, chaps," the Russian said.

Chapter 32

THE THREE AMERICANS TURNED as one, jerking their grease guns to the firing position. The Russian officer held up both hands.

"Please, gentlemen," he said. "The last I heard, we are still on the same side."

"Who the hell are you?" Mac demanded.

"Captain Valentine Valery of the Soviet Army." Valery clicked his heels and offered a mocking salute.

"You don't talk like a Russian," Roy said. "You talk like a Brit."

"A result of my English schooling, I fear," the Russian said. "My father was a diplomat stationed at our London embassy." He addressed Mac. "I assume you are Captain MacAuley of the OSS, yes?" Mac nodded. Valery turned to Harry, who still held the spear. "And that being held by— I'm sorry, we haven't been introduced."

"Harry Herschel," Harry replied. "Lieutenant." He nodded at Roy. "Staff Sergeant Damper."

Valery nodded, acknowledging the introductions. "And that being held by Lieutenant Herschel, I assume, is the object we all were sent to retrieve—the Spear of Destiny."

"We?" Mac said.

"You three, and my men and me," Valery said. "Obviously, you won the race."

"Your men?" Mac eyed the Russian. "Where are they?"

Valery glanced around the cellar. "Oh, they're around." He looked back at the OSS team. "Please, gentlemen, lower your weapons. My pistol is holstered, my rifle is slung, and my hands are empty. I come as an ally, not an enemy. What's important is that we keep the spear out of the hands of Himmler and his lot."

Roy and Harry looked at Mac. He sighed and nodded. They lowered their grease guns.

"Thank you," Valery said. "Now may I suggest we move our meeting outside this oppressive castle? The stench of the SS permeates the air."

Valery led the way up the stairs to the courtyard. Mac expected to see Russian soldiers, but the courtyard was empty. He left his weapon's barrel pointing at the ground, but his fingers tightened around its pistol grip. Mac figured Valery's men were outside the castle, possibly waiting to jump them. But outside the arched entry sat only their jeep.

"Where did you say your men were?" Mac asked.

"I didn't," Valery said.

"How many of you are there?"

Valery sighed. "Sadly, not as many as I started with."

They reached the jeep. Roy climbed in and fiddled with the radio. Mac opened the footlocker and placed the True

Spear inside. As he did, they all heard vehicles approaching. An American jeep appeared in the brick drive, followed by a deuce-and-a-half truck.

"More of your lot," Valery muttered. "I say, this does complicate things."

The vehicle stopped several yards away. Soldiers leapt from the truck bed and spread out in a firing line. An officer climbed from the jeep and stared at the OSS team and Valery before unzipping and removing his combat jacket. The other soldiers did the same.

"Krauts!" Roy slipped into the front passenger seat and jacked a round into the .30 caliber machine gun.

"I'd say it just became even more complicated," Mac said.

No one moved. The Germans stared at the Americans and the lone Russian, and they stared back. Gun barrel stared at gun barrel. At last, he German officer removed a white handkerchief from his pocket, raised his arm and, waving it like a flag, marched toward the jeep.

Harry spotted the runes on the officer's tunic. "Mac, they're SS," he whispered.

Mac nodded but said nothing. He seemed to be doing something inside the footlocker. Finished, he closed the locker and walked toward the German. "Gibst du auf?" *Are you surrendering?*

Steiner paused, a bemused smile forming on his lips, then continued walking. "No, I'm not," he said in perfect English. "I came to talk. And I speak English, as you can hear."

"American English, too, it sounds like," Mac said.

The German nodded and stepped forward, replacing the handkerchief in his tunic. "I spent my childhood in the States," he said, "until my parents brought us all back to the Fatherland."

"Major Steiner, I presume," Valery said.

Again, a bemused smile formed on Steiner's lips. "A Russian who speaks English, and British English at that," he said. "Have we met?"

Valery shook his head. "I know only your reputation." He glanced at Mac. "Major Steiner was with the group of Germans who infiltrated your lines in the Ardennes dressed in American uniforms." To Steiner, he asked, "I assume all your men speak English as well?"

"Like me, most are German immigrants who returned to Germany," Steiner said. "But we've got one or two Americans, too, former Bund members who came to serve the Führer."

"Traitors, you mean," muttered Roy.

Steiner shrugged. "We think of them as heroes of the Reich."

"That's enough," Mac snapped. "You two can form a foreigners-who-speak-English club later. What do you want, Steiner?"

"The same thing that brought you to Castle Wewelsburg," Steiner said. "The spear."

"Spear?"

"Captain, don't screw around with me," Steiner said. "There's only one thing in Castle Wewelsburg that would interest both the Americans and Russians. I don't know how either of you found out about it, but that's the Spear of Destiny. And since you were placing something in that footlocker attached to your jeep as we pulled up, I assume you found it." He looked to Valery. "The Yanks beat you to it?"

"I'm afraid so," the Russian said.

Steiner turned to Mac and said, "Captain, it's been a long war for all of us. And it's almost over. There's no reason to continue the killing. The spear has no military significance—it has no significance to either of your countries. But it's part of our Germanic heritage." Steiner tapped himself on the chest. "And it has particular sentimental value to the SS. So, please hand the damn thing over and we can all go home."

Mac said nothing. He simply shook his head and said, "Spear?"

Steiner sighed. "If I have to walk back to my men without the spear, I will have them open fire on you," he said. "Then I'll just take the damn thing."

Mac looked at Valery. The Russian simply raised his eyebrows. He looked at Harry and Roy, took a deep breath, and let it out. His shoulders sagged.

"Okay," Mac said. "You win. Harry, give him the spear."

Harry hesitated before opening the footlocker and removing a display case. Light from a dying sun glinted off its intact glass.

"Not that one," Mac said. "Give him the real one. The one with the broken glass. You heard the kraut major, he doesn't like to be screwed around with."

Harry stared at Mac, his eyes pleading.

"Do it, Harry!" Mac said. "That's an order."

Harry swallowed hard, set the case down, and removed the one from Himmler's safe. He handed it to Mac and whispered, "Mac, please …"

"Shut up," Mac said. He turned and handed the case to Steiner. The German eyed the broken glass and looked at Mac for an explanation. "We had to blow the safe open. It cracked the glass."

Steiner nodded and without another word, turned and walked back toward his men. With the spear in one hand, he reached into his pocket with the other, withdrawing his handkerchief and holding it at his side.

Roy stiffened. His trigger finger tightened. "Mac?"

"I see it," Mac said.

Valery gave him a curious look. "When he drops the kerchief," Mac explained, "they'll open fire."

"Just like Vercors," Roy muttered. "Must be the same bastard."

Steiner took his time returning to his men as he anticipated the look on the faces of the Amis and the Russisch when they realized they were about to die. He reached the side of his jeep, turned around, wiped his face with the handkerchief, and let it slip from his hand.

"Ogon'!" Valery screamed. *Fire!*

Machine gun and rifle fire belched from the cupolas of both towers. Roy opened up with the .30 caliber, while Mac and Harry sprayed bursts from their grease guns. Steiner and his men fell like bowling pins without firing a shot.

"Prekratit' ogon'!" Valery yelled, waving his arm. *Cease fire!*

The firing stopped. Mac dashed up to Steiner's jeep and looked at the SS officer, his mouth turned down in a scowl. Steiner looked up at him and coughed up blood. "Ours is not to reason why," he mumbled in German. "Ours is but to do and …" He coughed up more blood, then closed his eyes and lay still.

Mac squatted next to Steiner, grabbed his gray tunic, and lifted his head off the ground. "Don't you die yet," he yelled. "I'm not finished with you." He shook the German, but there was no life left in him. Mac stood, still grimacing, and kicked the corpse in the ribs. "That's for Vercors, Steiner," he yelled. He smashed his boot heel into the German's face. "And that's for Summersby!"

MacAuley stood over the body, breathing hard, his body heaving. Roy came up to him. "Kick him again, Mac. Get it all out." Mac turned on him, his face a twisted mask of rage. "You want to shoot him again?" Roy asked. "Empty an entire mag into him? How about that? That'll make you feel better, won't it? Or maybe we cut off his head and stick it on a pike like they did in the old days. I bet we can find a pike somewhere in this castle—whatever the hell a pike is."

Mac's face relaxed, his breathing calmed. He glanced at his radio operator. "Why don't you shut the hell up?"

Chapter 33

"MAC ..."

Mac turned from Roy. "Yeah, what is it, Har—"

A half dozen Russian soldiers stood abreast of each other in a semi-circle around the three Americans, their weapons at the ready. Valery stood in front of them, holding the spear and its cracked display case. The Russian officer smiled.

"There is a saying in England—I believe you have it in the States, too—that possession is nine-tenths of the law," Valery said.

"Tell that to any burglar caught with the goods," Roy muttered.

Valery shrugged.

"What now?" Mac demanded.

"What now?" Valery looked surprised at the question. "Why, we leave, of course. Courtesy of Major Steiner's American vehicles."

Mac said nothing, but his face revealed doubt.

Valery shook his head. "Captain MacAuley, if I intended to kill you and your men over this ..." He looked at the religious icon with disdain. "... this talisman, I could have done so much sooner. My men were already in the towers when I approached you in the cellar. We watched from a distance as you spoke with what I assume was a prisoner of some sort who told you where the spear was located. I decided to let you do … what's the saying?" Valery paused, thinking. "Ah, yes, to do the heavy lifting."

"How generous," Mac said, his voice flat.

"We Russians are a naturally generous people," Valery conceded. "Which is why I am saying we can all go home now. The war is all but won. Consider this—" He turned and swept an arm toward the dead SS troops. "Our last skirmish of the war."

Mac stared at the Russian, his eyes angry, but said nothing.

"Well," Valery said. "So be it." He turned and snapped out an order in Russian. His men fell out and started boarding the 2.5-ton truck. A noncom climbed behind the wheel of the jeep. Valery sat in the passenger seat and placed the spear and its case on his lap. "I would say I hope we meet again, Captain MacAuley, but if we did, it would no doubt be on opposing sides."

Valery smiled and flipped Mac a cocky salute, then nodded to his driver.

The engines started and the jeep and truck backed down the brick drive. Mac stood motionless, glaring after them. When they disappeared and Mac heard the motors fading in the distance, he turned and walked back to the jeep. Roy sat in the driver's seat, his forehead resting on the wheel. Harry was leaning with his elbows on the footlocker, his face buried in his hands.

"What's with you guys?" Mac asked.

Harry looked up, his blood-drained face screwed with incomprehension. "What? What's with us? You just gave up and let Valery take the Spear of Destiny! What do you mean *what*?"

"No, I didn't," Mac said.

"Didn't what?" demanded Harry.

"I didn't give up, and I didn't give Valery the True Spear." Mac shooed Harry away from the footlocker and opened it. He removed the undamaged case they took from Himmler's office and held it up. "This is the real spear. When everyone was gawking at the krauts coming up the drive, I switched them. *You*, Harry, damn near gave Steiner the real spear." He tossed Harry the spear. "Check it out."

Harry stepped away several feet and turned his back. He removed the spear and scrutinized it. After several minutes, he turned, grinning.

"You son-of-a-bitch," he laughed, "you did! You switched the spears!" He held the spear aloft. "This is the True Spear!"

☼

It was growing dark, and Mac decided to hole up for the night inside the castle. "Too close to the war's end," he

239

explained. "Too many Nervous Nellies out there shooting at any shadows they think they see."

They took the jeep into the castle courtyard and found some wood to build a small fire. They scavenged some bottles of wine from Himmler's personal wine cellar and dined on C-rations by the glow of the fire. The true Spear of Destiny sat on a small table near the fire, the flames glinting off its unmarred glass. Harry started laughing, laughing hard and uncontrollably. Without knowing why, the other two started chuckling.

"What the hell is with you, Harry?" Mac asked, trying to stifle his laughter long enough to swallow his mouthful of ham and beans.

"I just can't get over how you tricked them," Harry said.

"Tricked them?" Roy said, laughing. "Tricked us, too, damn you!"

"When you handed Steiner what I thought was the real spear, I thought I was going to cry," Harry said. "When you let Valery take off with it, I really did cry."

"Ain't no German alive Mac can't outsmart," Roy said between guffaws. "Russki, too." He took another bite of his rations and chewed, sobering as he did. "You know, there's one thing I don't understand," he said, wagging his spoon at Mac. "How did that Russki know your name?"

Mac washed down the last of his ham and beans with a swig of liberated wine. "You know," he said, nodding. "That's a damn good question. A damn good one."

Mac took the first watch, letting his partners get some much-needed sleep. When he figured Harry and Roy were asleep—easily determined with Roy because of his snoring—Mac picked up the spear and removed it from the case. He studied it in the fire light, holding it one way, then another. With a glance toward the others, he slipped out his Fairbairn-Sykes dagger and went to work on the lance head. When he finished several minutes later, he replaced the spear in its box and set it back on the table.

He picked up a wine bottle, walked to the castle entrance and, leaning against its stone wall, stared into the surrounding darkness. Somewhere in the distance, artillery boomed. He thought about what Roy said, took an angry swig of wine, and wiped his lips with his sleeve.

"A damn good question," he repeated to himself.

PART THREE

The Voyage Home

Chapter 34

COLONEL FENDER WAS BESIDE himself with laughter.

The Parsifal team returned to Patton's headquarters the next morning and reported to the OSS leader. Fender's eyes scrutinized the Longinus spearhead, then turned to Harry. "You're sure?" he asked. "You're sure this is the True Spear?"

"Yes, sir," Harry said. "I verified it twice."

Fender cocked an eyebrow. "Twice?"

Harry and Roy launched into a duet describing how Mac fooled both the SS major and the Russian captain, Valery.

"Fooled them? Fooled us, too," barked Roy between guffaws.

Fender himself was wracked with so much laughter he couldn't hold the spear any longer. He set it on his desktop and flopped into his chair, wiping tears of glee from his eyes. He struggled to speak between ripples of laughter and waved Mac toward his cabinet where he kept his scotch. "Mac … drinks. Drinks!"

Grinning, Mac placed Himmler's faux spear on the colonel's desk, retrieved the whiskey and four glasses. He poured everyone a generous share of Fender's booze. Harry took the offered glass but hesitated.

"Isn't it a little early for drinks?"

"Oh, hell, lieutenant, it's five o'clock somewhere in the world!" Roy said, sparking another round of laughter, which ended with everyone drinking.

Once he regained his composure, Fender said, "You know, boys, I always thought this was a wild goose chase—at least after you returned from Nuremburg empty-handed. But Patton was determined to get his hands on this …" He placed a hand on the True Spear. His voice lost its mirth. "You know, he really believes in its legend."

Fender removed his hand, but stared at the spear, lips pursed in thought. After a moment, he shook his head and humor returned to his voice. "But then, he believes he's the reincarnation of a Roman Legionnaire or some other such nonsense. Anyway, once I told him Harry's hunch about how the spear might be hidden in the Berghof, Patton was adamant you find it. I had no choice but to send you off searching—"

"So, you issued us unending orders so we'd follow up any other hunches Harry might have," Mac said.

Fender smiled and nodded. "That's about it, Mac."

"Pure fools," Harry muttered.

"What's that, lieutenant?" Fender asked.

"Oh, it's part of the Parsifal and Percival stories, sir," Harry explained. "Only a fool who is pure at heart stood a chance of finding the Grail and the Spear of Destiny."

"I can only speak for myself," Roy said. "I may be a fool, but I ain't been pure since my last year in high school."

More laughter. Colonel Fender said, "Well, drink up, gentlemen. I need to report this to the general."

With a final bottoms-up, they finished their drinks and prepared to leave the colonel's office. Mac reached for Himmler's fake spear, but Fender stopped him.

"If you don't mind, Mac, I'd like to keep this," he said. "A sort of memento of the whackiest OSS mission I ever oversaw."

Mac grinned and chuckled. "Sure, sir. Sure."

☼

The war in Europe ended seven days later.

Grand Admiral Karl Dönitz, Hitler's appointed successor, agreed to surrender to the Allies as Russian troops swarmed through Berlin's streets. Back in the States, soldiers, sailors, marines, and airmen joined civilians in celebrating "Victory in Europe." Fender rewarded Mac, Roy, and Harry for their successful mission with a two-week leave in England. But there was still a war ongoing in the Pacific, and Captain Raymond MacAuley was preparing to join it.

"What is it with you, Mac?" Roy demanded. "You got a death wish?"

Mac looked up from the typewriter on which he was typing his transfer request. He had returned from London, determined to stay in the war.

"No," Mac said. "But we've still got OSS units fighting in Burma and China. What good am I sitting around here?"

"Jesus, Mac," said Harry, "you've already done your part. You've been in combat since Africa. You should be rotating home."

Mac resumed his typing and didn't answer the question.

Roy threw himself into a chair and lit a cigarette. "You know what, Harry? I think that whole Parsifal thing got to Mac. You know, the part about being a pure fool. He's taken it to heart."

Mac glared at Roy but continued typing.

"You know, maybe you're right," Harry said. "Maybe we're all pure fools. What do you say we join Mac in the CBI Theater?"

Mac's typing ceased. He leaned back, scowling at Harry. "You'll do no such thing." Lighting a cigarette, he said, "This is my decision. I don't need you traipsing after me, getting in the way."

"Or getting ourselves killed?" Roy interjected.

Mac scowled at Damper again. He pulled the paper out of the typewriter and patted his pockets for a pen. "You got a pen?"

Roy pulled a pen from a pocket and waggled it just outside of Mac's reach. When MacAuley tried to grab it, Roy returned it to his pocket. "I'm not letting you use my pen to sign your death warrant."

Mac sighed and glanced at Harry, who shrugged. "Sorry."

The door to their quarters opened and Colonel Fender stepped in.

"At ease," he said, even though none of the three Parsifal members moved to stand at attention.

"Colonel, do you have a pen I can borrow?" Mac asked.

"Ah, sure." Fender reached into his coat pocket and handed Mac a pen.

"No!" Roy shouted.

"Don't let him do it, colonel," Harry pleaded.

Puzzlement crossed Fender's face as he held up his hands, palms up. "What?"

"Don't pay them any attention, colonel. They're still drunk from R&R." Mac scratched his signature onto the document and handed the pen back to Fender. "Thank you, sir." He handed Fender the signed transfer request. "This is for you, sir."

Fender took a minute to read the document, nodding as he did so. "So, you want to transfer to one of the OSS detachments in Burma or China?"

"Yes, sir."

Fender's brow knitted as he looked at Mac. "You don't think you've done enough already, Mac?"

"I simply think I can still do more, sir," Mac answered.

Fender reread the request, scratched his forehead, and sighed. "Denied."

"What?" blurted Mac.

Harry and Roy responded in unison. "Yes!"

"Colonel, I have the right to request a transfer," Mac protested.

"Yes, you do," Fender said. "But you specifically requested a transfer to another OSS command."

"So?"

Fender crushed the request into a ball and hurled it into a waste basket with more force than necessary. It bounced out of the basket and rolled along the floor. Before Mac could retrieve it, Roy leapt on the paper wad like a cat, tore it into small pieces, and dropped them into the basket.

"So …" Fender drew out the word, his voice edged with anger. "The OSS is being disbanded."

Chapter 35

BY AUGUST, MAC WAS back in Bavaria, promoted to major, and reassigned to the Counter-Intelligence Corps to ferret out any remaining Werewolf partisans and other dead-enders, as well as any communist moles the Russians may have infiltrated in the American zone. Mac's fluency in the German language made him valuable to CIC's efforts, as the Americans had recruited many Germans to aid their work. Reinhard Gehlen, a former German lieutenant general and head of German military intelligence on the Russian front, was among those hired. Gehlen hired more ex-Nazis to work for his organization, including former Gestapo agents and SS officers. None of that endeared Gehlen to Mac, who had been on the receiving end of Gestapo and SS tactics.

Mac's continued quest for a transfer to the Pacific Theater met with repeated denials. His knowledge of partisan tactics and his language skills were too valuable to the CIC. And now there was news that an end to the war with Japan was in sight. The U.S. Army Air Force had dropped an unbelievably powerful bomb on the Japanese home island, devastating a city called Hiroshima. Facing such power, the

Japanese warlords would surely have to surrender. It was just a matter of time.

But what caught Mac's eye was not the news about the Hiroshima bombing, but a message saying an American Army lieutenant named Horn—a member of the Monuments Men seeking stolen art treasures—had discovered a cache of lost Holy Roman Relics in Nuremburg. Some of the Imperial Regalia—including the Spear of Destiny— were found sealed in a secret bunker beneath a bakery. Horn found the rest in another underground shelter below an elementary school only a thousand yards from the first bunker. Horn, it seemed, had developed the same intel on the relics' location. Despite the success of the Parsifal mission, General Patton ordered Horn to retrieve them. The Allied command was preparing to return the relics to the Hofburg Palace in Vienna from which the Nazis had stolen them.

A young captain poked his head into Mac's office. "Hey, major. The boys are going down to the O-club to celebrate the war ending. Want to come?"

Mac looked up from the report he was reading. "No thanks, Richards. I've got work to do."

The captain looked at his watch. "Hey, it's way past the quitting hour, sir. You deserve some R&R. The war's all but over."

"The war's not over until the shooting stops, Richards," Mac said a little too sharply. Easing his voice, he added,

"Go on, have fun. I've just got some tidying up to do. Maybe I'll meet you all there later."

"As you wish, sir," Richards said.

Mac lit a cigarette and stared at the wall. Patton had the True Spear. It didn't seem right to Mac that the Hofburg Palace should get the fake lance his team found and left in Nuremburg. The museum had hired Harry's father to authenticate it, after all. Patton knew the spear in the Nuremburg bunker was a replica, and Mac was certain the general wouldn't tell anyone that, not as long as he held the real thing. Mac frowned and snubbed out his cigarette.

"Goddammit," he muttered as he slipped on his Ike jacket and overseas cap. He stomped out the door and slammed it behind him.

Mac drove his jeep aimlessly through the dark streets of Bad Tölz. Thick clouds obscured the slivered moon and the jeep's headlights were still blacked-out slits. He considered keeping his promise to Richards and joining his fellow officers to celebrate the bombing of Hiroshima, but his mood was sour, and he didn't feel like celebrating. To his surprise, Mac found himself parked near Flint Kaserne, the former Waffen SS training school that Patton—as Bavaria's military governor—took over for his headquarters. Lighting a cigarette, Mac stared at Kaserne's large arched entrance bordered by two fat, round turrets without noticing the soldiers coming and going from the headquarters building.

"Mac? Is that you?" a familiar voice asked.

Mac roused himself from his fugue and found Colonel Fender staring at him from a few yards away.

"By God, it is you, Mac!" Fender stepped lively toward the jeep as Mac climbed out and saluted. Fender returned the salute, then shook MacAuley's hand. Referring to Mac's new rank insignia, he said, "Say, Mac, those oak leaves look good on you."

"Thank you, sir."

"So, what are you doing hanging out here in front of HQ?" Fender asked.

Mac shrugged. "Slumming, I guess."

Fender glanced at the Kaserne and nodded. "That's as good a description as any. I tell you, Mac, you're lucky your CIC unit isn't billeted here. It's a goddam madhouse here."

"Madhouse?"

"Patton's off his rocker," Fender said, leaning closer and lowering his voice. "He's not doing anything to help the locals or the displaced persons as military governor. He's still commander of Third Army, too, but he's never here."

"Patton doesn't live here?"

"Nah," said Fender. "He's got a palatial house out on Lake Tegernsee that used to be owned by the guy who published Hitler's *Mein Kampf* book. Spends most of his time there cooking up schemes to start a war with Russia."

"*Another* war?" Mac couldn't believe anyone would want another war after seeing the destruction wreaked by the last one.

"Unbelievable, right?" Fender took out a pack of cigarettes, offered one to Mac, then took one himself. "He's talking like Hitler—the Jews are the problem and Russians are all subhuman. The krauts are the only good people left in Europe. That kind of crazy stuff. The division surgeon thinks the old man is suffering from too many blows to the head from falling off horses. He had a name for it which I don't remember, but he said it was like a boxer being punch drunk."

Fender blew out a lungful of smoke and shook his head again.

"You won't believe this. On the other side of the lake from his residence, there was a full Waffen SS division in the Kreuth Mountains. Not fighting, but still fully armed, waiting to surrender. And Patton actually talked about using them to march on Moscow."

"You're kidding," Mac said.

"I wish I were, Mac," Fender said. "There are rumors Ike's had it up to here—" Fender held his hand above his head. "—with Patton's follies and is considering shit-canning him."

"Ike couldn't do that," Mac said. "Patton's too popular."

"Not among the Allied leaders, Mac." Fender dropped his cigarette and squashed it with his boot heel. He sighed. "I know, I'm talking out of school. But Patton's crap is getting out of control." He fell silent, shaking his head, before continuing. "Ah, dammit. Let's change the subject. How's CIC treating you?"

"I don't like some of the company I'm keeping," Mac said.

"Gehlen and friends?" Fender surmised.

Mac nodded. "Any chance of reassignment back to your command, sir?"

Fender grimaced as he shook his head. "OSS is being eaten up by other commands and agencies. Wild Bill's trying to keep some kind of organizational structure because there's a rumor of a new, more centralized intelligence operation coming down the pike. It's probably pie in the sky, but we still need something like that in the coming years. That or we end up with another Pearl Harbor."

The colonel glanced at his wristwatch. "Oh, hell, eighteen-thirty hours," he said. "I've got to run, Mac. I've got a date with a pretty little fraulein." He held out his hand and Mac shook it. "It's great to see you again, Mac. Next time you're out wandering around, stop in and see me. Unlike Patton, I am billeted here. The gate guard will tell you where to find me."

"I'll do that, colonel," Mac said. "Where'd you say Patton was billeted?"

"Lake Tegernsee, about twenty kilometers southwest from here," Fender said, already walking away to his appointment. "Why? You thinking of paying Old Blood and Guts a visit?" Fender's laughter echoed through the empty street.

Mac lit another cigarette and climbed back into the jeep. He thought about Fender's last remark, a sly grin forming on his lips. "You never know," he muttered.

Chapter 36

HE WORE A GERMAN army officer's uniform with riding boots over cavalry pants, an officer's greatcoat hung over his shoulders, and a peaked cap. All rank insignia had been removed. The MPs manning the gate at Patton's palatial estate did not consider his dress unusual; most of the German men in Bavaria had little more than the remnants of their uniforms to wear. What was different was his bearing. Standing erect and confident, he delivered himself before the guards as if he were on an inspection tour. The man eyed the guards through a thin veil of smoke rising from a cigarette held in a short, black holder clenched between his teeth. He removed the cigarette and its holder with his left thumb and forefinger, the palm up, and stood before the MPs as if waiting for an introduction.

"May we help you, sir?" said the senior-most soldier, a corporal.

The German looked down his nose at the guard. From beyond the guard post came the sound of music and the chatter of people mingling. The man held his right hand out, palm up, indicating the music.

"Ich bin eingeladen," he said. *I am invited.*

"I'm sorry, sir," the corporal said, "but I *nein sprechen Deutsch*."

The German glared at the corporal before turning to the second MP, a private.

"I think he's saying he's invited to the general's shindig," the private said.

"Oh." The corporal picked up a clipboard with a leaf of papers attached. "May I have your name, sir? I mean *namen*?"

Glaring at the MP again, the German snatched the clipboard and leafed through its pages. He pointed to a name and slapped himself on the chest. "Das bin ich." *That is me*.

"Ah, General Storch?" the corporal read.

"Ja, das bin ich," the German said.

"Very well, sir," the corporal said. "Please go on in and enjoy the evening."

The general marched into the villa as if on a parade ground.

"Goddam krauts," the corporal complained. "They act like they won the damn war."

"Probably one of those Prussian guys you hear of," said the private. "All starch."

"More like SS," muttered the corporal. "Old Blood and Guts acts like he's all gaga over them."

A young German girl in a maid's outfit greeted the former German general at the door and offered to take his hat and coat. Once she had them in hand, she directed him through double doors leading to the reception.

"Bitte, wo könnte ich mich erfrischen?" the German asked. *Please, where might I refresh myself?*

The maid directed him up a winding flight of stairs and to the first door on the left on the second floor.

"Danke," he said and climbed up the steps with deliberate aplomb.

Reaching the washroom, Raymond MacAuley closed the door behind him and let out a deep sigh. He felt like he'd been holding his breath for the past ten minutes. Apparently, arrogant bluster could persuade American soldiers just as it did Germans.

Mac locked the door, splashed some water on his face, and took out a hand-drawn map of the premises. For the past week and a half, Mac had been studying Patton's villa. In a municipal office, he found a copy of the original architectural drawings, including the interior layout of the two-story mansion. He rented a rowboat and—with the help of a set of fine, German-made binoculars—spent two days observing the comings and goings around the villa from the lake and identified the second story suite of rooms Patton used as his office and living quarters.

Fender was right, Patton had chosen one of Bavaria's most opulent estates to serve as his residence. Set back from the lake and shaded by trees, it sported a swimming pool and a bowling alley. That surprised Mac—he never figured Germans bowled. A small dock jutted into the lake, with two sailboats tied to it. Max Amann, Hitler's former sergeant in the first war and publisher of his autobiography, purchased the villa before the war, largely with profits from *Mein Kampf*. The neighborhood Amann selected was quite exclusive; one of Amann's neighbors was Heinrich Himmler and his wife.

When Mac learned Patton was hosting a reception for the local gentry, he saw his chance to get to the spear. All he needed to do was bluff his way into the party. He acquired a German officer's uniform from a POW camp and removed its insignia. Then, by pretending not to speak English and snatching the invitee list from the flustered MP corporal, he was able to find an attendee who suited his assumed persona. Now all he had to do was get into Patton's quarters, find the True Spear, and get out before the real General Storch arrived.

Mac oriented his hand-drawn map of the upper floor and collected his thoughts. Unlocking the washroom door, he peered out. The hallway was empty. Patton's quarters were across the hall and down four doors. He stepped out into the hallway and, still strutting like a Prussian prince, approached the door to Patton's rooms. It was locked, as he expected. It took him only seconds to open it with a pick and stepped inside.

Now came the hard part—where would Patton keep the spear? Hitler locked what he thought was the genuine spear into a concealed wall safe. Himmler, too, kept the True Spear in a safe. Mac began checking behind each painting, curtain, and wall map for a hidden safe, but found nothing. He slipped into the general's bedroom and repeated the process with the same result. Finding nothing, he checked each drawer and wardrobe in the bedroom. Still nothing.

Mac returned to the office, intending to check the drawers there.

Then he saw it.

The Spear of Destiny sat in its case on Patton's desk. Mac had been so certain the spear would be hidden, he hadn't even glanced at the desk earlier. Of course, he now realized a man with Patton's immense ego wouldn't hide the spear; he'd have it prominently displayed so his admirers could see it. Hell, he probably planned to mount it on a lance and carry it into battle against the Russians.

MacAuley's plan was simple—grab the spear, return to the washroom, and toss it out the window into the bushes below. Afterward, he would retrieve his coat and hat and, mumbling some excuse about not feeling well, leave the building and recover the spear from where it lay in the bushes.

He picked up the spear and headed for the door, but something stopped him. Stepping back to the desk, he switched on a lamp, withdrew the spear from its display case, and scrutinized it. The mark he made on the spear the night they spent at Wewelsburg Castle was not there.

What Mac held—what Patton had on display—was not the True Spear.

Chapter 37

COLONEL FENDER WAS TYPING a report to William Donovan, the chief of the OSS, on his futile attempts to keep the agency's northern European operations intact when someone knocked on his door. "Enter!"

Mac opened and walked in smiling.

"Mac!" Fender stepped around his desk and welcomed his old friend. "What are you doing here? Slumming again?"

Mac chuckled. "Something like that." He opened a bag and removed a bottle. "Harry, Roy, and I drank enough of your hootch. I thought I'd return the favor. Afraid it's only schnapps. Couldn't find any scotch."

"Well, that's fine, fine," Fender said, fetching two glasses off a shelf. "I'm actually developing a taste for it."

Mac poured them each a good measure, and they sat, Fender behind his desk and Mac in a padded lounge chair. "Did I come at a bad time, colonel?" he asked, pointing to the files and typewriter on Fender's desk.

"No, no," Fender said, pushing the folders into a pile. "Just letting Wild Bill know the OSS in Europe now virtually exists in name only."

"No luck holding it together?"

Frowning, Fender shook his head and took a drink. "It's amazing. Before the war, everyone in Washington believed spying was something gentlemen didn't do. Some people actually said that, you know. 'Gentlemen don't read other gentlemen's letters.' Now everyone wants their piece of the action." He took another sip, then looked at MacAuley with a wistful smile. "We did some good work, Mac."

"Damn good work," Mac conceded.

"Well, as they say, 'No good deed goes unpunished.'" Fender raised his glass in a toast. "To the good ol' days, may they never be forgotten."

"To old, departed friends," Mac added.

After drinking to the toasts, Fender asked, "What really brings you around, Mac?"

Mac smiled and scratched an ear. "I was curious how your date with the fraulein went?"

"Oh, that." Fender gave Mac a sheepish smile. "It didn't go anywhere. Turns out she has a husband in a POW camp in the States. Captured in North Africa."

"And?" Mac prodded.

"And gentlemen may read other gentlemen's mail, but we don't boff their wives."

"Since when?"

"Since I learned she had three kids, all of them living with her." They laughed and Fender proffered his glass. "Come on, how about a refill?"

Mac refilled the colonel's glass. Fender leaned back in his chair, eyeing MacAuley. "Really, Mac, what really brings you here?"

Mac grimaced and took a deep breath. "You remember what you asked me last time we saw each other?"

Fender pondered the question, then shook his head. "No. What did I say?"

"You asked if I was planning to visit General Patton at his Lake Tegernsee villa," Mac said.

"Did I?" Fender shrugged. "So?"

"So, I did."

Fender set his drink on his desk and leaned forward. "You what?"

Mac described how he gained entrance to Patton's villa. "I wanted to steal the spear," he explained. "It didn't seem right that he had the True Spear and was sending the fake spear we found in Nuremberg to the Hofburg Palace museum in Vienna."

"Oh, Mac," Fender sighed, "you always had an overactive sense of right and wrong. You know that's not always good for a spy. Did you find the spear?"

Mac nodded. "I found *a* spear," he said. "I did not find the True Spear."

"What are you talking about, Mac?" Fender asked. "Harry identified it. How would you even know if it was real or not?"

"The night we camped over in Castle Wewelsburg," Mac explained, "while Harry and Roy slept, I put my own mark on it so *I* could identify it if I needed to. The general's spear doesn't have that mark."

Fender now leaned back and eyed Mac. "Are you sure?"

"Positive," Mac said.

"Then—then who has the True Spear?"

Now it was Mac's turn to eye Fender.

"You do," Mac said. "You asked to keep Himmler's fake spear as a souvenir, remember? You gave the fake to Patton and kept the True Spear."

"What the hell are you talking about, Mac?" Fender's voice rose, indignant. "Why the hell would I do that? I don't believe in that rubbish like Patton."

Mac rose and paced the floor. "No, but Patton does, and you didn't want him to have it any more than I do. Neither of us trust him with it."

"That doesn't mean I didn't give him the correct spear," Fender said. "I'm a soldier. We both are. We follow orders, even if we don't like them. Just like you and your team did when ordered to find the goddam spear."

Mac lit a cigarette and nodded as he exhaled, leaving a ragged cloud of smoke swirling around him. "There was something else eating at me." He tapped his head. "Something back here. That Russian officer I tricked, Valery. Remember we told you about him?"

Fender steepled his fingers and nodded. He was guarded as he answered. "Yes."

"I couldn't stop wondering how he knew my name, and that we were after the spear like him," Mac said. "A report from the Brits came across my desk. It seems when Patton announced the discovery of the Holy Roman Relics—including the Spear of Destiny—Stalin guessed the one Valery brought to him was a phony. The good Captain Valery figured there was a firing squad in his future, or worse, a one-way trip to Siberia. So, he defected to the British Zone where, I understand, he is being very cooperative."

Mac stubbed out his cigarette, finished his drink, then lit another smoke. "A couple days ago, I drove over to the British Zone and had a talk with Valery. According to what he was told, Russian intelligence had agents high up in both the OSS and the German SS. They knew about Himmler's plan and our plan to retrieve the spear."

"You're saying we have a leak—here in our operation?" Fender asked. He rubbed his chin. "If that leaks out, what's left of OSS is finished."

"It doesn't have to leak out, colonel," Mac said, "if you turn yourself in."

Fender froze for a moment, then glared at MacAuley.

"What the hell, Mac?" he demanded. "First you say I stole the Spear of Destiny, and now you're saying I'm a commie spy?"

"I remembered that during the Spanish Civil War, you were a big supporter of the Loyalist side. The Russians supported the Loyalists."

"And the Nazis supported the Nationalists," Fender said. "So what?"

"You must have made some contacts with Soviet intelligence," Mac said.

Fender was quiet for a moment, then he took a deep breath and sighed. He nodded. "Yes, I did, Mac. But I'm no commie. I'm an antifascist. I wanted to make sure Hitler didn't get his hands on the True Spear—or Patton, for that matter. It's too damn dangerous."

"I believe you, colonel," Mac said. "So, where's the spear—*the True Spear*?"

Colonel Fender took a key from his pocket and reached down to open a drawer. He froze as Mac opened the flap on his holstered .45 caliber service automatic.

"I'm simply getting the spear," Fender said. He continued opening the drawer, removed the True Spear, and placed it on his desk.

Mac removed the lance blade from its case, took it to a light, and examined it. He turned and nodded. "It's the True Spear."

"Of course, it is," Fender said. "What are you going to do with it?"

"Return it to the museum, I guess," Mac said. "Maybe hand it over to Ike and let him do it."

"And me?" Fender asked.

Mac considered that for a while. "I'm with counter-intelligence now. It's my job to turn you in."

Fender closed his eyes, sighed, and nodded.

"But I'm not," Mac said. Fender's eyes popped open. "I said it before, I don't believe you're a commie. Technically, you were helping an ally. Turn yourself in and I think the brass will want to sweep it under the rug."

Fender nodded again. "Thank you, Mac."

"But don't tell anyone about this," Mac said, placing the spear and its display box inside the bag he brought the schnapps in. "At least not until I figure out how to proceed."

Chapter 38

IT WAS 9 A.M. on a chilly December morning when General George Patton stepped out of the old hotel in Bad Nauheim, Germany, that served as his new headquarters and residence. Two months earlier, General Eisenhower—tired of Patton's provocative press statements and his failure to follow orders to de-nazify Bavaria—relieved Patton of command of the Third Army and his position as military governor of Bavaria. Patton's new command was the Fifteenth Army. The Fifteenth was an army in name only, a collection of military historians and clerks whose job was to write the official history of the U.S. Army's war in Europe. It was, Patton believed, his ultimate fall from grace. In one more day, he would leave Europe for the U.S. with thirty days' leave. He was not planning on returning. Instead, he would resign his commission.

Despite the dark cloud he'd been living under, on that winter day Patton was in a good mood. He and his chief of staff and old friend, Brigadier General Hobart "Hap" Gay, were going pheasant hunting. Patton took a deep breath of crisp air and rubbed his gloved hands together in anticipation. For the first time in weeks, it felt good to be alive.

Sergeant George Meeks, Patton's Black personal valet, approached the general carrying a valise. "General, your case, sir."

"Thank you, George," Patton said. "Place it in the trunk, would you?"

"My God, Georgie," admonished Gay, "you're not actually taking work with you, are you? It's your last day before going on leave."

Patton smiled and chuckled. "It's not work in there, Hap," he said. "It's my good luck charm, and I'm not letting it out of my sight until I'm back home in the States."

"Well, okay," said Gay. "But that must be the biggest rabbit's foot I've ever seen."

Patton laughed and slapped his friend on the shoulder. "Come on, let's get going. Those pheasants aren't going to wait for us."

They climbed into the back seat of an olive-drab 1939 Cadillac limousine. Stiff red flags bearing four stars jutted from each front fender. It was a hundred miles to where they intended to hunt, and it was too cold for an open staff car. A following jeep carried their shotguns and a gun dog.

Nearly three hours later, they were on the autobahn a bit outside Mannheim, waiting for a train to pass. When the last railcar crossed, Patton's limo moved forward as an oncoming army 2.5-ton truck turned left in front of them. A collision was unavoidable.

Both Gay and the driver saw the oncoming truck and braced themselves. Patton, staring out the side window, deep in his own thoughts, did not. "Georgie, lookout!" cried Gay, but it was too late.

The impact crushed the front of the Cadillac and shoved it down an embankment, throwing Patton and Gay to the floor. When the limo came to a rest, the driver leapt out and threw open the rear passenger door. Patton lay on the floor conscious but with blood flowing from a head wound. Hap Gay huddled over him, uncertain what to do.

"Georgie, are you all right?" Gay asked.

Patton didn't answer for a moment, then he muttered, "I think I'm paralyzed. I can't move." After another moment, he added, "This is a helluva way to die."

A Red Cross girl serving doughnuts not far away saw the crash and summoned the battalion surgeon from a nearby combat engineer unit. The doctor at once realized Patton's neck was broken and ordered an ambulance to take the general to an army hospital at Heidelberg, twenty miles away.

As medics and MPs and others clustered around the rear doors of the Cadillac preparing to remove Patton's limp body, a lone MP stepped to the rear of the vehicle, opened its trunk, and removed the general's valise. As he closed the trunk, a master sergeant stopped him.

"What are you doing there, soldier?" the sergeant demanded.

"I'm with the general's security team," the MP said. "I'm securing his papers. I'll follow the ambulance and secure them in a safe at the hospital."

"Good idea." The master sergeant nodded. "Carry on."

The MP placed the valise in his jeep and waited for the ambulance carrying Patton to pull out. He followed the ambulance as it sped along the autobahn, sirens screaming. In Heidelberg, the ambulance pulled into the hospital's driveway, but the MP jeep didn't follow. It continued on for several minutes before pulling to the side of the road. The soldier climbed out of the jeep, removed his white MP helmet and brassard, and tossed them into a field. He pulled two gold oak leaf rank pins from his pocket and secured them to his shirt, then fitted an overseas cap on this head.

Major Raymond MacAuley opened the valise and removed Patton's mock Spear of Destiny, what the general considered his "good luck charm." There was nothing else in the bag, so Mac hurled it into the field with the MP helmet and armband. When finished, he sat in the driver's seat with the fake spear next to him, lit a cigarette and contemplated his next move.

He thought about disposing of the fake spear the same way he did the helmet and valise. It was doubtful anyone would find it any time soon. If someone did, they would have no idea what it was. Or would they? That was the problem. There were too many fake Holy Lances floating around. For the same reason he followed Patton on his hunting trip, intending to steal the phony lance head, he had to make sure no one found it now that he had it. If Patton started flashing his spear copy around, insisting it was the True Spear, questions would start circulating about the authenticity of the spear in the museum in Vienna. If someone stumbled onto the spear in the field and recognized it, the same thing would happen.

He made his mind up and flicked the cigarette into the road, started the jeep, and headed back toward Bad Tölz.

Twelve days later, Patton succumbed to his injuries. In the intervening time, Mac drove out to Lake Tegernsee and parked along its shore not far from the estate where Patton had lived. From a rucksack, he took out Patton's replica and broke it into its various components—the gold and silver sheaths, the embedded nail, and the blade itself. As he walked along the shore, he tossed each piece into the lake as far as he could, walking and tossing, walking and tossing.

When he finished, Mac lit another cigarette and trudged back to the jeep, lost in thought. He only had a month left in Germany, having received orders sending him back to England. From there, he would board a troopship back to the States. He still had the True Spear he'd taken from

Fender, unable to decide what to do with it. Originally, he intended to return it to the Hofburg Palace. But that presented the same problem Patton's possession of the imitation spear did—questions about which was the real spear and where had it come from, and who had had it—questions he didn't want asked or answered.

As he reached his jeep, he turned and took a last, long look at the lake. The water was placid, glinting with moonlight. His CIC unit recently received intelligence indicating the Nazis had dumped caches of weapons, maybe even gold bullion, into the lake to hide them from the Allies. Eventually, the Allies would drag the lake or send divers down to search it. Mac regretted not being around when they did. It would be interesting to see what they found, if anything.

Suddenly, like an image in a telescope coming into focus, he knew what he had to do and why.

Chapter 39

THE LUXURY OCEAN LINER Queen Mary steamed through the bleak North Atlantic fog. She still wore her wartime coat of gray, which matched the dank January mist surrounding her. That drab paint and her unmatched speed had earned her the sobriquet "The Gray Ghost" during the war. Too fast for convoys or German U-boats, she ranged across the Atlantic and Pacific oceans alone, carrying tens of thousands of Allied troops, appearing and disappearing like some phantom of the sea.

Her speed was of no use to her now. Peacetime rules of navigation required her to proceed through the fog at a cautious pace. For most of the thousands of American servicemen aboard her, that was a great disappointment, slowing their return to their homes and loved ones. For Raymond MacAuley, it made no difference. He wasn't eager to reach the States. He had other things on his mind. At that moment, though, he was just hungry.

He had been waiting in line for dinner in the officers' mess for twenty minutes. Dining aboard the troopship Queen Mary had none of the elegance of dining on the ocean liner Queen Mary. The thousands of soldiers, sailors, and airmen crossing on her stood in long lines on her mess desks, received their meals on metal trays, and more often than not, ate their meals while still standing in line to exit the mess deck.

"Mac?" A familiar voice called out. "Hey, Mac!"

Several officers turned, looking for whomever was calling their name, but only Mac recognized the face belonging to the voice. Harry Herschel, now wearing captain bars, was pushing his way through the crowded mess, slipping from sight before reappearing again like a man struggling to stay afloat in a stormy sea.

"Harry!" Mac called out, waving his arm.

Harry's face appeared a few feet away, then disappeared again. He reappeared a few feet farther away, losing ground to the human tide. "Mac!" he cried out.

"Harry," Mac hollered, "meet me on the promenade deck, starboard side, under the forward funnel in one hour! Harry, did you hear me?"

Harry's face surfaced once more, still farther away. "Yes! Promenade deck in one hour. Forward funnel!"

With that, Harry disappeared.

An hour later, Harry was wending his way through the crowded promenade deck when a voice above him called his name. "Up here, Harry."

Mac's face appeared over the gunwale of a lifeboat hanging in its davit. Harry jumped and grabbed the gunwale, pulled himself over it, and slid into the partially uncovered lifeboat. He looked around. A single GI-issue right-angle head flashlight lit the interior. Mac sat at the bow where the canvas cover was unlashed and pulled back. A rucksack sat next to him. An ash tray made from the bottom half of a beer can sat on the other side of him.

"Nice place you have here, Mac," Harry said.

"Only first-class accommodations for the OSS," Mac said. "Congratulations on your promotion."

"Same to you, major," Harry said. "Are you living in this boat?"

"Nah, I climb in here to get away from the crush," Mac said. "It's too crowded below decks and too crowded above decks. I have an agreement with one of the ship's crew members. He keeps everyone else out of the boat."

"How'd you come to that agreement?"

"I bribed him with a bottle of scotch I got in England," Mac said.

Harry laughed. "You don't still have that footlocker from the jeep, do you?"

"Let's say I came prepared." Mac opened the ruck and revealed two rectangular boxes bearing the imprint of a Scottish distillery. He opened one box, removed the bottle, and produced two ceramic coffee cups bearing the emblem of the Cunard-White Star Line. "I stole these from the mess deck."

Mac poured each a drink. "So, *Captain* Herschel, what have they had you doing these many months?"

"Well, *Major* MacAuley, they had me translating for the war crimes trials in Nuremburg," Harry said. "I even met Hermann Göring. I told him I saw him once in Berlin before the war. He made a joke about not looking like the same man because of all the weight he lost since the surrender. What about you?"

"CIC," Mac said with obvious distaste. "Working with a bunch of so-called *ex*-Gestapo hunting down Russian stay-behind agents."

"You ever hear from Roy?"

Mac chuckled. "Roy went back to England, met a pretty young French-Canadian nurse serving in the Red Cross and got married. They're already back in Quebec making babies."

They drank to Roy's marriage, and Mac asked, "What are you going to do when you're back in the States?"

Harry shrugged. "Finish my doctorate. Get some boring professorship somewhere teaching history."

"Boring?"

"Anything after the OSS is going to be boring," Harry said. "And you?"

"I'm not sure," Mac said. "I might stay in the army. Colonel Fender said there's serious talk about forming a new centralized intelligence service. Maybe I can get my foot in the door."

"How is the colonel?"

Mac frowned and poured more scotch into each of their cups before explaining the last stages of the hunt for the Spear of Destiny—how he marked the True Spear when they camped at Wewelsburg Castle; how the Monuments Man Horn found the Holy Roman Relics in Nuremburg and returned them to the museum in Vienna, along with the counterfeit spear from the bunker; how he'd snuck into Patton's residence near Lake Tegernsee and discovered the general's spear was also bogus; how he'd deduced Fender had the True Spear with the help of the Russian defector Valery; and how he'd snatched Patton's phony lance and disposed of it in Lake Tegernsee just to tidy things up.

"Jesus, Fender was a commie spy?" Harry said.

"He prefers the term antifascist," Mac said.

"What'd they do to him?"

"He took my advice and turned himself in," Mac said. "No one wanted to make a big deal out of it—technically, he was aiding an ally—so they let him resign his commission. But he'll never work for the government again."

Harry fell silent, thinking over everything he'd been told. After a minute, he looked up suddenly. "Wait. What about the True Spear? Who has it now?"

"I do."

Mac reached into the rucksack and took out the remaining bottle box. He opened the end and slid out the Spear of Destiny. Harry grabbed the lance and held it under the glare of the flashlight. Picking up the flashlight, he turned his back to Mac and examined the spear. When he finished, he turned to Mac.

"It's the real thing," he said.

Mac nodded and took the lance from Harry's limp hand.

Harry slowly emerged from his fugue. His eyes narrowed as he looked at Mac. "What do *you* plan to do with it, Mac?" he asked.

"Originally, I was going to return it to the museum," Mac said. "That's what I told Fender. Then I started thinking—myth or no myth—it's too dangerous even for a museum to keep." He tapped his forehead. "I kept asking myself all these what-ifs."

"What-ifs?"

Mac sipped his scotch and sorted out his thoughts.

"You once said maybe just believing in the spear's legend could spur a man on to greatness," Mac said. "But what if the legend *is* true? What if the Spear of Destiny does convey some sort of power on the person who owns it? That's what-if Number One. Hitler never had the real spear—he thought he did, but it was fake. And yet he managed to conquer most of Europe only *thinking* he had it. But what if he had the actual spear and its legend was true? That's what-if

Number Two. What unimaginable greater evil could he have done?"

"But Hitler didn't have the True Spear," Harry said. "Himmler did."

"And Himmler was in the line of succession to replace Hitler," Mac replied. "Hitler's own generals tried to kill him with a bomb. What if they succeeded, but their coup failed? Himmler—the man holding the real Spear of Destiny— would come to power and then what? Those are what-ifs three and four, by the way."

"But Mac, it's only a legend," Harry protested.

"You thought it important enough to find the spear to alert the brass about its location," Mac reminded him.

"Because it's a historic, Biblical relic," Harry said, "not because it's supposed to be a magical talisman of power. That's a myth. You said that yourself, Mac, when we first met."

"I did." Mac nodded. "But think about it, Harry. Hitler thought he had the spear, and now he's dead. Himmler did have the spear, but he lost it—"

"We stole it from him."

"—and now he's dead—killed himself after Berlin fell," Mac said. "Patton thought he had the real spear, and now he's dead—exactly as the myth predicts." Mac took a long drink from his cup and shook his head. "I don't know if the legend is true. But if there is a chance, the barest chance it is, then I think the True Spear is too dangerous to leave lying around, even in a museum. What if the next person who owns it is another power-hungry nut job like Hitler, or Stalin, or Patton?"

"Or you?" Harry asked.

"Or me," Mac agreed. "Or you."

Harry fell silent again. He stared into the dark shadows of the lifeboat as if he was looking into the abyss. Finally, he grabbed the scotch bottle, poured another drink, and swallowed half of it at once. "So, what are you proposing to do, Mac?"

"I was talking to the ship's navigation officer earlier today. He mentioned we are currently sailing over one of the deepest parts of the northern Atlantic. So deep, even our best submarines can't dive that far."

"Too deep to retrieve something that fell overboard?"

Mac nodded.

"Why didn't you throw it into Lake Tegernsee like you did Patton's copy?"

"Lakes occasionally dry up," Mac said. "Besides, there were plans to search the lake for a cache of gold we were told the Nazis dumped into it."

"So, you're planning to drop it overboard?"

"I was," Mac said. "But when I saw you on the mess deck, I realized it was really a two-man job."

Harry leaned back and stared at the black nothingness of the fog-shrouded sky. The True Spear was a priceless relic. How could they toss it overboard, lost to history forever? But there was sense in what Mac said. Just believing in the legend—believing he possessed the True Spear when he didn't—allowed Hitler to conquer so much of Europe. What if the legend were true and another Hitler gained possession of the real thing? What havoc could he wreak? After a few minutes, he sighed, looked at Mac and weakly nodded.

Mac smiled. "Good."

With the spear concealed beneath Mac's jacket, they climbed out of the lifeboat, bulling their way through the throng of servicemen to the ship's railing. The green starboard running lamp above them illuminated the swirling gray water below. Mac removed the spear from his coat and held over the sea in one hand. Harry also gripped the lance head.

"On three," Mac said. "One … two …" He glanced at Harry, who nodded back at him. "Three!"

The True Spear of Destiny, the lance the Roman centurion Longinus used to pierce the side of Christ as he hung on the cross, dropped through swirls of fog and disappeared beneath the surface of the Atlantic Ocean.

Author's Note

THIS IS A WORK of fiction, but its plot was inspired by historical facts. After annexing Austria, Germany's Nazi government confiscated the Holy Roman Relics from the Hofburg Museum in Vienna and placed them on display in Nuremburg. When Allied bombers began pummeling German cities, the relics were placed in a secret underground bunker in Blacksmith's Alley, near Nuremburg Castle, for safekeeping.

In the last weeks of the war, an American interrogator named Lt. Walter Horn received information from a German POW on the secret location of the relics cache. General George Patton, who was a renowned "souvenir" collector, ordered Horn to retrieve the relics. Horn located some of the relics, including the Spear of Destiny, in the Blacksmith's Alley bunker. The true story of the young lieutenant's search for the remaining relics has all the hallmarks of a mystery novel. Once retrieved, Patton resisted returning the relics to the museum in Vienna until ordered to do so by General Dwight Eisenhower, the supreme Allied commander.

Patton's erratic post-war behavior, as described in this book, has been recorded by military historians. At one point, Eisenhower and the senior Allied leadership became so concerned by his behavior, an army psychologist was secretly attached to Patton's headquarters staff to keep an eye on him. Unfortunately, his behavior ultimately led to his losing his beloved Third Army.

As I said before, this is a work of fiction, but in writing the story, I tried to adhere to the historical timeline of the last days of WWII as best I could.

About the Author

MARTIN ROY HILL is the author of two national award-winning series—the Linus Schag, NCIS, thrillers and the Peter Brandt mysteries—as well as the USCG DSF-Papa sci-fi thrillers, *Eden: A Sci-Fi Novella*, and a collection of short stories, *DUTY*. He is a former journalist and national award-winning investigative reporter for newspapers and magazines. His nonfiction work has appeared in *Reader's Digest*, *LIFE*, *Newsweek*, *Omni*, the *Los Angeles Times*, and many others. His short fiction has appeared in *Alfred Hitchcock Mystery Magazine*, *ALT HIST: The Journal of Historical Fiction and Alternate History*, *Nebula Rift*, *Mystery Weekly*, *Crimson Streets*, and others.

He lives in San Diego, California, with his wife, Winke, son, Brandon, and their three feline overlords.

Follow Martin Roy Hill on:

Facebook: https://www.facebook.com/Martin.Roy.Hill

Twitter: https://twitter.com/MartinRoyHill

Website: https://www.martinroyhill.com

If you enjoyed reading this book, please leave a review on Amazon.com, Barnes & Noble, Goodreads, or your favorite review site.

9 798218 182496